Plotlands

Carol Fenlon

Published in 2016 by FeedARead.com Publishing

A CIP catalogue record for this title is available from the British Library.

This book is a work of fiction; any resemblance to persons living or dead is entirely coincidental.

Acknowledgements

Grateful thanks are due to members of Edge Hill University's Narrative Research Group for their invaluable feedback and constructive criticism.

I am also indebted to Rhona, Jackie and Lizzie, friends and fellow members of the Society of Authors for their patient readings and suggestions which have helped to shape and polish this book.

Special thanks go to members of Skelmersdale Writers' Group for their feedback and in particular to Elizabeth Brown and Phil Hollingsworth for their help and advice on preparing the book for publication.

Finally a big thank you is due to Mark,John and Will, my Welsh friends, and to all the people at Rhuddlan community centre with whom I have spent enjoyable Sunday breakfasts, mining their knowledge and memories of the area in which the book is set.

Books by the same author:
Fiction:
Consider the Lilies (Impress Books, 2008)
Triple Death (FeedaRead 2016)

Non-fiction:
*Skelmersdale: A New Town in the Making: Part One,
From Fantasy to First Brick* (Beacon Press, 2015).

For my Welsh grandson
Ted Jr.

Contents

The Soft Throat of the Sand

Graham came to Plotlands after he murdered his wife.
He got away with it on a plea of self-defence.
Everybody had known Sheila for a bully and the jury
felt sorry for him.

Still, after all the dirty washing in the newspapers
and the silences when he entered the local shops, he
couldn't very well stay in Birkdale. His daughters
wouldn't speak to him and his firm advised him to take
early retirement.

The house was cheap and when Graham went to
view it, he realised why. It wasn't actually a house but a
1930s prefab with a number of ramshackle extensions
in a variety of styles. At some point in its history
someone had attempted to give it the appearance of a
bungalow with a few coats of pebbledash and paint but
now it just looked sad and weary – a bit how Graham
felt. It stood on a large plot, big enough to grow flowers
or vegetables or keep a few chickens or tinker with old
cars and motorbikes. Evidence of such hobbies he could
see all around in neighbouring yards.

Graham liked what he saw. He liked the converted
railway carriage on the plot next to Gracelands, as his
prospective home was inaptly named. He liked the

scrubby, wandering paths between the homesteads and the straight and narrow road that ran from the main north Welsh coast road down to the sea. Best of all he liked the bleak, muddy shoreline with its abandoned lighthouse and the humps of carelessly thrown sand dunes that separated Plotlands from the endless beach with its shivering sands and the distant sea. He didn't care so much for the huge gas terminal that skulked in the distance to the right of the beach path, but you couldn't see that from Plotlands itself and there was something comforting about the flare that flamed at night, almost like a replacement for the beam of the abandoned lighthouse.

It rarely rained in Plotlands, or so it seemed, and he delighted in walking along the beach path on fresh, cold mornings and again in the afternoons after a day of scraping off the pictures of Elvis which papered the walls of Gracelands. Should he rename the bungalow? This was a question that sometimes occupied him on his walks. It stopped him from thinking about Sheila, from re-living over and over the feel of her throat pulsing under his fingers like a frightened animal, how hard and tough it had been under the flabby skin; how surprised he'd been by its texture, so surprised that he'd forgotten to let go in time. Alone on the winter landscape he wondered if she could see him enjoying his freedom, and how she would feel about it but he soon learned to keep his wits about him as he walked when one day his foot sank ankle deep in the quicksand that he hadn't noticed.

Only later did he see the warning notice on the beach information board that told you where the patches of quicksand were and what to do if you got stuck. Don't panic. Lie down and wriggle slowly backwards. He filed the information away in his brain.

10

It wouldn't do to get stuck there. People did walk dogs along the dunes but few came out to the beach in the winter months. There weren't even many residents in winter, another plus for Graham. Many of the houses seemed to be holiday homes, their owners only visiting for the occasional weekend to check on their places. The mini-amusement arcade was closed up and the chippy opened only at weekends.

The few people who lived there permanently obviously all knew each other and soon they all knew Graham too. It could have been a problem but there was something about Plotlands that made you feel you could be whoever you wanted, do what you liked and no one would bother you. No one asked questions, although they might gossip behind your back. He'd heard them in Milly Pink's shop talking about people he didn't know when he went in for milk and his newspaper.

Graham used his middle name, Arnold, and his surname was too common to be picked up in connection with the murder. Jack, the motorbike freak who lived in the railway carriage next door, called him Arnie and cracked jokes about the Terminator but otherwise left him alone. People were friendly but private and after only a few weeks, Graham felt himself unfurling like a flower in the sun, something he'd never experienced before.

There were no rules at Plotlands beyond minding your own business and live and let live. The clubhouse near the beach stayed open for as long as people wanted to drink, not that Graham had yet entered in, but he could hear the karaoke, often until two in the morning, the singing getting progressively worse as the vocalists got drunker. The café opened when its owners felt like it, when they observed sufficient hikers and dogwalkers dotting the dunes. There was no pressure to join groups, make friends or engage in conversations. Graham had always been a silent man, mostly because first his parents and then Sheila, had never stopped talking at him and silence was now ingrained, dialogue a fearful thing, beset with pitfalls – a bit like the Plotlands beach.

Graham began to be happy. Even when Spring came and he started to realise that his peaceful idyll would be shattered by the clouds of holidaymakers already beginning to descend on the large caravan site further up the road, he saw that he could preserve his anonymity. He would be able to lose himself in the crowds, withdraw into the privacy of his home, which was now becoming a pleasantly cluttered place to live, stamped with his own personality, but then Shazza dropped into his life.

No one knew Shazza's story. She appeared at Marita, the old prefab directly opposite Gracelands one fine weekend in April and embarked on an aggressive clean-up with much banging of brooms and flapping of cloths.

'All right?' she grinned at Graham when he emerged for his afternoon walk. 'I'm Sharon. Everyone calls me Shazza.'

'Arnold,' Graham said. Feeling constrained to be polite he went across to shake her hand. Close up she was older than he'd first thought. In her tight tee shirt and leggings, he'd taken her for twenty-something but close up, her skin texture and the lines on her face put her closer to his own age.

'It's me aunty and uncle's place. He died last month. She can't get around by herself. I offered to bring her but she don't want to come no more.' She moved the wad of gum she was chewing round her mouth as she talked and the words came in short bursts as she energetically wiped the large window fronting the bungalow.

'Will you be staying?' Graham ventured, finding it difficult not to stare at her heaving bosom as she worked. So much of it was on show.

'Not sure. It's a terrible mess.' She dropped her cloth into the bucket beside her, leaned against the wall and squinted at Graham. 'I used to come here a lot with them when I was little. Not so much later, but now and again. I got a bit of a soft spot for the place. Not seen you before?'

Graham was fascinated by the workings of her jaw, her red lips and her large even teeth chomping on her gum. His penis twitched unexpectedly. 'I moved here about four months ago.'

'Like it?' She felt in her jeans pocket, pulled out a pack of cigarettes and lit one, offering the pack to Graham.

'I don't smoke, thank you. Yes. I mean, yes I do like it.' Her eyes were green. Strands of hair lay over them like the fringe on a Yorkshire terrier. She had a lot of bright blonde hair thrown up like a country and western singer. It gleamed in the sun. How slippery it would be in his fingers. She also had a soft, white throat. Graham put his hands in his coat pockets.

'Going to the clubhouse tonight? Not much else to do round here.' She sucked on her cigarette, opened her mouth to let out the smoke and smiled at him. Graham's penis made its presence felt and he was glad he had zipped up his coat.

'Yes all right,' he said, his mind pre-occupied with this unusual activity down below. It had been dormant for a long time. Later, he began to think with sinking heart, how he might be storing up trouble for himself.

Alarmed, he consulted Jack.

'Marty's dead?' Jack was sobered enough to separate himself from the old Goldstar he was working on. 'Poor old Rita.' He put down the crank cases he had just removed and wiped grease from his blackened hands onto his blackened jeans. 'Marty and Rita – they've been coming here since way back.'

'I think she's moving in.' They both stared across the road at Shazza. Now that he was at a distance in the shared male camaraderie of Jack's scrapyard garden, Shazza's cleaning presence took on the appearance of a major offensive – a female invasion of their peaceful life. They sat in the sun watching her over mugs of oily tea.

'Don't know her,' Jack said. 'Seen her a couple of times with Rita and Marty so she's not a squatter. Poor old Marty eh? Wonder what happened.' He didn't wonder enough to go over and ask Shazza. It wasn't the Plotlands way. You waited for things to come to you.

But Shazza hadn't waited. She'd asked him straight out. Was it a date? Graham pondered this on his walk, pushing away his apprehension at the prospect of an evening in the clubhouse with a strange woman.

He needn't have worried. After only an hour in the bar, she led him back to her house to share a bottle of wine and a pizza. Graham looked down at his hands sliding through her waves of shiny hair, her head bobbing up and down on his penis. Sheila would never have consented to such a thing. It was a new experience for him and his ecstasy was doubled by the thought of Sheila angrily (or perhaps enviously) watching somewhere in the ether.

Afterwards they lay face-to-face on her aunt's dilapidated sofa and his fingers strayed to the pulse at the base of her neck. The feel of it beating there transcended even the delight of the orgasm that had rattled through him shortly before.

Within a couple of weeks Graham's solitary life had turned upside down. His lonely walks were curtailed. There were always other things to do, shopping trips with Shazza to nearby Prestatyn or Rhyl, and occasional outings by train to Chester or even Liverpool. Then there were so many things he could help her with; clearing Marita's overgrown garden, decorating, repairs – the list was endless.

There were nights out too, not just to the clubhouse but meals in restaurants, spicy foods that gave him indigestion which he cheerfully endured for the promise of stroking her white throat and her wonderful breasts when they got back to her bungalow. For a while he moved in a dream but he came down to earth with a bump one morning when on his way to buy his morning newspaper at Milly Pink's shop, three people including Milly herself asked him how Shazza was keeping. With a sense of imprisonment, he realised he'd become half of a couple.

'She's got you by the trousersnake, man,' Jack said, offering him a grimy gingernut to go with his tea. 'You'll be marching down the aisle before you know it, if you're not careful.'

Graham looked glumly at the boat engine Jack was currently taking to bits. No boat could be launched from the Plotlands beach, but then Jack was always doing things up to sell at the car boot sale at Rhuddlan.

'Been married before?' It was the first direct question about his past that Jack had asked him and it brought home the seriousness of his situation.

'Yes,' he said absently, thinking how Shazza was always at him, trying to find out about his pre-Plotlands existence and he realised that sooner or later, if things continued, he would have to tell her about Sheila and then his secret would never be safe. And things did continue because his penis still hammered in his pants whenever she was near, but gradually the pressure of her demands began to outstrip the delights of the nights he spent in her company. Just now and then, he caught in her tone a nagging whine that reminded him of Sheila. Each time he heard it he wilted a little more until the clear realisation came that if he didn't take steps to free himself it would be too late.

'I'm going to spend tomorrow walking, take a picnic.' He began confidently enough but just seeing her expression made him waver.

'But you promised to paint the bathroom.' There it was again, that whingeing tone, her red lips pursed in a sulky pout.

'It can wait. The weather's fine for walking.'

'I'll come with you.' She pressed closer against him on the sofa.

'I want to go by myself. I need to be alone sometimes.'

'Aw c'mon Arnie.' She turned her face up, puckering her mouth to be kissed but he could see how the lines round her eyes tightened, her lips tensed like a tight arsehole. Her angry body was overpowering, he wanted to push her away. His hands slid round her neck, how neatly it fitted in them. The pulse at the base of her throat fluttered. It was like holding a little bird, feeling fear in its fragile bones. That's what he wanted, to be in control. If only she would do as he wanted.

'Arnie, you're hurting me.'

She couldn't keep quiet, couldn't stop whining. He'd thought she was different. She just had to learn, accept he was master. 'Show her who's boss' Jack had said. Then everything would be all right.

16

Pain bit him, ripped his grip from her throat. He came back to her claws tearing at his fingers. He stared, horrified, at the red marks burning the white skin of her neck. She pushed him away, got up and stumbled to the bathroom, choking and retching.

What could he say? He left, his head thundering with what he had done. Was this how it was to be, never to be able to trust himself with a woman, perhaps not with anyone? He was a werewolf here among the nice people of Plotlands; gentle eccentrics like Jack; retired old folk like Marty and Rita, delivering their precious little niece into the hands of a waiting monster. Now everyone would know what he was really like. Shazza wouldn't be one to keep quiet. He could see them all whispering in Milly Pink's shop, the gossip rippling out across the uneventful life of Plotlands, no doubt getting more and more distorted as it spread. He tossed all night, delirious with nightmares that paled before the waking reality, while the one remaining picture of the King watched from the wall opposite the bed.

Dawn found him on the beach, a black figure in a grey seascape. He looked down at his hands – killer's hands. Everywhere he could hear it, the trees whispered it, little birds chirped it. The seagulls screamed over his head, 'killer, killer.' That's what he was. He had read somewhere that the first killing was the worst, after that it got easier, mundane even.

He'd thought he could escape but now he saw he'd been handcuffed to death ever since he'd killed Sheila. Even though the court had set him free, he'd crossed a line that set him apart from the rest of the world. Death was everywhere, even here at Plotlands; the scream of a rabbit torn by a fox; the ripping of fish guts by the cruel beaks of seabirds; Marty – dead and gone, his existence marked only by half the name of a ramshackle prefab; even Elvis, King now only on paper to be scraped off and taken to the tip to rot back into the ground. Like Plotlands itself, slowly decaying into the sandy soil. Where nothing had once been, nothing would be again. Graham himself sank, his right foot and half his leg sliding into the quaking sand.

The advice on the noticeboard came back to him. 'Lie down and wriggle slowly backwards.' How undignified. He was the one in control here. He lifted his left leg, making his right sink further and struggled to get the left leg to join it. He slipped down the soft throat of the sand until it swallowed him to the chest. He could feel his heart beating like a little bird inside the warm grip of the sand. He would not lie down. He folded his arms over what remained of his breast.

Fat-Bottomed Girls Are Bad For You

Jack sat outside Dunroamin on an old oildrum topped with a dirty cushion and watched Shazza sweeping her path. The woman was a fucking cleaning freak and vicious with it, you could tell by the way she attacked the dirt with her broom. Look what she'd done to poor old Arnie.

He'd never have fallen into the quicksand like that if he hadn't been wandering round with his head in a whirl. It was her fault, flashing her tits and ordering him about till the poor bastard didn't know if he was coming or going. Milly Pink at the shop reckoned he'd committed suicide. It'd come out in the local papers after he died, that he'd killed his wife before he'd come to Plotlands. It was a surprise but Jack had known there was something. There always was something. The way some people talked, you'd have thought he was a fucking mass-murderer but anyone who really knew Arnie (or Graham as it turned out he was really called), could tell he was just a victim, a man who couldn't help hitching himself to women who would make a fool of him.

'Remorse – come here to die,' Milly Pink kept telling everyone. Fucking old drama queen.

Jack knew better, no one really wanted to die. He was afraid of dying, despite the rose-adorned death's head on the Outcast colours stitched on the back of his leathers. He still kept the jacket hanging behind his bedroom door, although he couldn't wear it any more.

The skull grinned at him faintly when he was in bed, reminding him of things he wanted to keep sacred and things he wanted to forget.

No, it was Shazza who had driven Arnie to his death. Jack glanced at the empty bungalow next door, the For Sale sign creaking in the stiff breeze blowing on from the shore. She'd been all right mouthing off to everyone about how he'd nearly strangled her the night before he died but she'd never mentioned how she'd been milking him for everything she could get, using her body that way that women did. She was doing it now, pushing her tits out and wagging her arse. He could see her giving him little sidelong glances and when she got to her gate, she stopped, smiled and gave him a wave.

It wasn't as if she was really interested; no one was interested in him any more; well who would be? If he wanted, he could go into Rhyl, pay one of the bored tarts from the rough end of the prom but why bother? He'd rather jerk off with the copy of Hot Babes that he bought once a month on his shopping trip to town. Hot Babes wasn't the sort of mag you could ask Milly Pink to order for you. He looked forward to getting his fresh copy, fucking sad though it was. He couldn't afford a computer and anyway wanking in front of a screen or talking dirty down the phone didn't compare to cosying up in bed with a full colour spread of Shania Silk and letting his fantasies loose where no one could see what he looked like.

Shazza wasn't his type anyway, too fucking skinny by half. He watched her light up a fag and lean against her gatepost. No arse to speak of, not like Gloria. He remembered the first time he saw Gloria's arse billowing out on either side of the saddle on the back of Lenin's bike. His mouth had watered. It watered now at the memory, even five years on. He'd known from that moment that he had to have her, but she was Lenin's old lady, any advance would be fraught with danger.

He'd had girls before, of course, lots of them in the ten years he'd run with the Outcasts. And he'd almost been married once in that old life full of regulations before he became one of the brothers. Maybe Roz had loved him but he felt suffocated. He knew she thought a qualified motor mechanic would be a good catch, knew he would end up tied up in mortgages and mouths to feed.

Luckily the Outcasts had rescued him and he'd experienced a rush of freedom that matched the feeling of riding with them until he began to realise that he'd simply swapped one set of rules for another. Still, there were lots of women and no strings attached. None of them had mattered until Gloria. She was an itch he just had to scratch.

If it had been anyone else, it wouldn't have been so bad but Lenin was the leader of the Outcasts. You'd wonder why, a runty little cunt like him, till you saw the look in his eyes and you realized the guy was mean. And he'd earned his place, always at the front of any battle. The previous leader, Big Benny had ended up in a nursing home after Lenin made his bid for the position.

But all that meant nothing to Jack after the sight of Gloria's giant peach bouncing wherever she went. From the front there was no hint, except perhaps a promise in the plump cushions of her lips. She was the biker's dream; sweet face, long dark hair, big bosom, narrow waist, wide hips, slender legs, but when she turned around, oh boy, everyone stood to fucking attention.

In the days of fairground freaks, Gloria would have been a prize attraction. Her arse swelled out from her body like an extra appendage, great twin globes threatening to burst the seams of her jeans. Jack absently rubbed his groin. Shazza was walking back to her door now, her thin buttocks barely creasing her jeans. Jack started to tinker with the Goldstar's carburettor. The engine needed a good clean. He would take it apart later.

He was eating his monthly fish and chip dinner at his favourite chippy on Rhyl promenade when they roared up and burst in like an invasion. Just the sound of the engines made the food clot in his mouth. The engines were bright and loud, Jap bikes at a guess, not the comfy wheezes of innocent vintage Brit enthusiasts out for a quiet afternoon and an ice-cream. Jack put down his knife and fork and tried to stop his hands trembling. He peered at their backs and his fear receded, just a bunch of no-name wannabes but they'd almost had him fooled with their aloof stances, gritty stares, the half-abusive chaffing of the girls behind the counter. Another look told him they were kids, eighteen, nineteen, half his age. Nothing to fucking worry about.

The pensioners eating their specials stopped and stared, before dropping their eyes back to their plates. The bikers filled up the spaces with their greasy, lively bodies, filled up the air with their smell of leather and oil, with their voices, their guffaws, displacing the regular eaters, changing the place and making it their own. Fat Frank, the owner, kept one wary eye from the doorway to the back room as the girls toiled with the gang's endless order, while the other gleamed with satisfaction at the ringing of the till. Jack felt himself in no-man's land until two bikers parked themselves in the seats at his table, when there were no other places left.

'Hey, man, you look like you should have a bike outside.'

'Not any more.' Jack looked away from their curious eyes and into his mug of tea.

'Oh yeah?' One of them tapped at Jack's oil-rimmed fingernails. 'Once a biker, always a fucking biker.'

'Still like to tinker – boats, engines – got an old Goldie I'm working on.'

'Them old bikes are shit. You wanna get something decent.'

Jack looked into the guy's blue eyes. His lank blond hair was tied back in a ponytail, showing off his angular cheekbones and jaw. 'You guys on a club run? Got a name?'

'Nah, just mates. Most of us are in the Dragon club.'

Jack kept a smile off his face. Fucking amateurs!

'I got a cousin in the Outcasts,' the red-haired one volunteered.

'Oh, they're bad dudes,' the blond one snickered. 'Nobody messes with those fuckers.'

Jack hesitated. He mustn't give himself away but he badly wanted to know. 'I used to know a girl who ran with them.' He made his voice casual. 'Her name was Gloria.'

'Gloria the legend?' The blond one sniggered again. 'The legend of the Big Bottom?' Jack wanted to smack him in the mouth. He held on tight to his mug. 'She got smashed up.'

Jack's insides dropped. 'Smashed up?'

'On the back of her boyfriend's bike.'

'Lenin?' The name crawled out of his mouth as he sat helpless.

'Killed instantly. Way to fucking go, eh? Pity he wrote the Harley off.' The blue eyes blazed at him, filled with ignorance.

'Gloria – dead?' His lips wouldn't make the words.

'Nah, she ain't dead,' the ginger one spoke up. 'She was in hospital for ages, dunno what happened to her after that. You knew them both then?' He lit up a fag casually but his eyes never left Jack's face.

'Only vaguely,' Jack said carelessly, 'a long time ago.'

'Hey, no smoking in here,' Fat Frank called from his hiding place.

'Fuck off you old twat.' Ginger gave him the finger and carefully blew a large cloud of smoke. Others in the group followed suit. Someone rolled a joint. The air turned blue and pungent.

'I'm calling the police,' Fat Frank said and ducked away behind the gaudy ribbon curtain.

'Time to split anyway,' said Ginger, standing up and kicking his chair away. 'They call me Rube,' he said to Jack, '– and you?'

'Phil,' Jack said, shaking the proffered hand. It was cold as a corpse.

'So long oldtimer, take my advice – get a decent hog, get back on the road, live the life.' He squeezed Jack's fingers so hard he felt his bones grate together. There was no friendship in the green eyes that bored into him.

Wanker! Fucking silly kids. How old did they think he was? It must be the crutches, or was it just that anyone over thirty seemed ancient to them?

The relief of empty space was physical after they'd gone, despite the mist of smoke that still floated near the greasy ceiling.

'Good riddance,' muttered Fat Frank, wiping down the counter as if to erase their traces. The pensioners nodded. Jack suddenly did feel ancient. He waited till the roar of engines dwindled to normal traffic noise before gathering his carrier bags, getting out his mobile and calling a taxi to take him home.

After that she was constantly in his thoughts, even in his dreams. She had been the fucking one. Every other woman he'd known tried to lead you by the fucking nose, or rather by the dick; after what they could get, trying to tie you down, get you under their fucking thumbs, turn you into a no-balls jelly, but Gloria was different, you could just be with her, be yourself, be in love with her but love was a word he'd avoided – then.

The Goldie wasted, untended in the early summer rain as he drizzled the time away at his window, dazed by the jigsaw pieces that danced in his mind. Lenin – dead, an empty space, an open door, into which he could maybe fit, but then she'd gone back to him after what happened; that rankled. She'd been his for that short time only and Jack the realist knew things didn't last but Jack the romantic clung to the promises they'd made to each other.

It was his fucking fault though, not hers. She wouldn't have had any choice after he'd run like the coward he was without a thought for her safety. It was surprising that bastard Lenin had taken her back. God knows what he'd put her through – beatings, humiliation? Jack had seen his handiwork often enough, hadn't he tasted it himself?

He'd agonised about it all those weeks he'd lain in hospital, his dread growing worse as the days passed without a visit from her. He planned how he would go back for her, tortured by fears of what was happening to her, but when it came to it, he couldn't. He'd seen his fucking yellow streak and so had everybody else.

So where was she now, what was she now – scarred, crippled, disfigured? Behind the stabbing images a horrid selfishness lurked. Physical deformity would make them equals. Perhaps she still had feelings for him; after all she'd been the one who had saved him that day. Did he have the courage to find her? Hope and despair swung him this way and that for days. Weeks passed while he sat immobile, wrestling his thoughts until sheer lack of food sent him hobbling out and onto the bus that would take him into Rhyl.

As soon as the taxi dropped him back home Shazza knocked at the door.

'Someone's been to look at the house,' she said excitedly, crowding herself into the tiny galley kitchen where Jack was unpacking his shopping trolley.

'What?' Jack's mind was still running on the enquiries he'd made in town about trains to Manchester. He reckoned Gloria had gone to ground there, gone back to her family in Wythenshawe to lick her wounds. She'd taken him there once to meet her mum and her sister Sarah in those heady days when they'd been full of plans for escape to a future together, riding away into a new life.

'It'll be nice for you if he buys it, another biker to keep you company.'

His attention snagged on her words. Cold clenched his stomach. 'What sort of biker?'

Shazza shrugged. 'I dunno. Big. Big beard, a Scouser.'

'What bike did he have?'

'I dunno. Big, nice bike, shiny, lots of chrome.'

Fuck, fuck, fuck. Terror coursed through him until he forced himself to relax. It could be anyone. Anyway the guy was only looking, probably wouldn't buy the fucking place anyway. Nevertheless, he felt uneasy that night, sleep sliding from him as he chased it, his dreams full of wild shapes and imaginings that lurked on the edges of his consciousness when he awoke and blighted the fine sunny day. Letting his mind fill with images of Gloria helped and as the day wore on he almost forgot about Gracelands' prospective buyer.

Two days later he went to Manchester. It was a convoluted trip involving a bus to Prestatyn, a train to Chester, then on to Manchester and finally a bus out to Wythenshawe. He was exhausted when he finally arrived, his crutches barely holding him upright but he couldn't bring himself to knock at the door of Gloria's mother's house and spent some time skulking by a lamppost a few doors down.

After a while the door opened and Gloria's sister Sarah came out with a pushchair filled with a fat baby in pink. Jack gawped. She'd been a skinny kid last time he'd seen her. Hadn't taken her long to start opening her fucking legs. She looked like a harassed mother of five rather than a teenager. She had none of Gloria's beauty, although there were similarities that twisted his heart, in her eyes, in the way she moved. She walked past him without a glance, fiddling with the carrier bags hanging from the pushchair until he whispered her name and she froze, recognition paling her face.

'You!' She glared at him. 'What do you want?'

'I heard about the accident,' he mumbled, unable to look her in the eye.

'Fuck off. She doesn't need you. Get lost.' She stalked away.

He watched her back. She had a nice neat arse, not at all like Gloria's. The front door opened again and he held his breath but it was Gloria's mother. She wasn't a bad old cow; he'd always got on all right with her. His spirits rose a little. Maybe she would help him.

'Hello Rene.' He attempted a smile.

'You've got a nerve, coming here after all this time.'

'I heard about the accident. I didn't know. I just wanted to see her.'

'You leave her alone. She's got a new life now, away from them bikers. Got a good job on Piccadilly station, her own house, a nice little car. She deserves it after what she's been through. It was all your fault.

'Well in a way, you done her a favour,' her voice softened. 'She weren't never the same after you, and that Lenin give her a dog's life. It were a good thing when he got killed but she went through hell; broken legs, fractured hip.' She looked at Jack's crutches then looked away again. 'She's made a good recovery. She's happy now.'

'She married? Got a boyfriend?' He held his breath. Please, fuck, no.

'Don't even think about it.' Her bright gold head nodded like a dandelion in the wind. She reminded him of an older version of Shazza.

'I…'

'Just leave her alone.' She stepped back and shut the door. He stood there for a while, conscious of her watching him from behind the lounge curtains, then he turned and made his way back to the bus stop.

Piccadilly station, she'd said. He scoured every inch of it; the ticket offices, the shops and cafés. 'Please God, give me a fucking break,' he prayed, hoping she wasn't hidden away in some invisible office in the bowels of the building. He found her on Platform Nine, checking the tickets of passengers for the London train. Her wonderful hair was confined in a bun, her curves hidden under a severe uniform but the clumsy skirt couldn't hide those fabulous buttocks. His hands remembered their contours as his eyes feasted on the swell of them when she moved. There was no sign of disability, disfigurement, nothing to show she had ever been injured.

Did he stare too much, or make some involuntary sound or gesture? She looked up and saw him. He saw the colour drain from her face, her dark eyes widen in shock and he melted away into the crowds.

All the way back the knowledge thrummed in his head. He could just fucking take her back. He'd seen it instantly as she looked at him. Despite his deformity, his treachery, love had shone out of her face. It had been too much for him, what a fucking dickhead he was walking away like that. He'd go back, in a day or so, give them both time to get used to the idea. Euphoria filled him with energy. He was going to get another chance. There must be a fucking God after all.

Darkness was falling when he got back to Plotlands and Shazza must have been waiting for him. As soon as he put on his lights, she was there, all agog.

'He's definitely buying it. A weekend place for him and his mates. He lives in Liverpool. His bike's a Harley Magician, custom chopper.' She beamed like a schoolgirl successfully reciting from memory. 'I told him all about you. He's dying to meet you.'

Gloria fled out of Jack's mind. He looked at Shazza's scrawny neck. No wonder Arnie had nearly strangled her. 'He tell you his name?' he managed to whisper.

'Pete,' she grinned.

Stupid, stupid fucking bitch. He resisted the urge to push her off his property, kick her skinny arse back to her own place.

'Was there anything painted on the bike, on the tank or anywhere, a skull, anything like that?'

'I dunno,' she was crestfallen at last. 'There was stuff on it but I can't remember…'

Pete? Could be any fucker. Jack tried to reassure himself without success. He couldn't settle to eat or watch TV. He sat outside on his oildrum, the Goldie looming out of the dark beside him like a faithful guard dog, and looked at the black windows of Gracelands. The night was still warm and all was quiet except for the odd squeal of a rabbit, distant music from the clubhouse and the far backdrop of the whispering sea.

When Jack went to bed he took down the jacket bearing his Outcast colours and hid it under his pillow. It could too easily be seen by any fucker looking through the window. Thoughts of Gloria and the new owner of Gracelands swirled through his brain, and when sleep came, he was back in the nightmare he'd tried to forget, the thing he was always running and hiding from.

From where he was lying on the floor, he had a bird's eye view of Gloria, her eyes staring in their sockets, mouth a great red scream, breasts bursting from her tee shirt as she struggled vainly in Lenin's grip, her arms pinned behind her while the Outcasts' leader looked on. The pictures kaleidoscoped as Lenin's bastard minions, Jack's erstwhile blood brothers, waded in with fists and boots, his body thudding backwards and forwards between them. Fuck, fuck, cunting, fucking, fuck. Jack's mind was beyond sensible thought and language as he tried to deal with each blow. At last there was a space, a silence. Lenin's face hung over him, grinning like the skull on the colours, as he blurred in and out of consciousness. Something else waved before his eyes, a great spanner and Lenin's mouth whispered words of menace. Jack couldn't make them out but he knew they were about revenge and dishonour.

'Fuck you,' he mouthed, although he had long since ceased to struggle.

The sound of the first crack seemed to be outside, like thunder till it was followed by the pain and although he'd stayed silent before, a scream tore out of him as long and as loud as the fart that came as he lost control. The shattering of his other knee was an anticlimax and his last clear vision was of Gloria on her mobile phone, calling the police, the call that saved his life.

They turned him over, his face smothering in his own blood as they tried to rip the colours from his back, the final dishonour, but the wail of approaching sirens prevented it and suddenly it was over and he was alone, lying in warm sticky wetness until blue flashing light and rough voices washed over him.

He woke to the warm sticky wetness of sweat-drenched bedclothes. He reached under the pillow and comforted himself with the cool touch of leather. They had taken his bike, his precious chopped Yammy, taken his self-respect, taken Gloria too but they hadn't got his fucking colours, although rightfully they were no longer his.

He kept thinking he would go for her, walk up and take her away from humiliating herself in that crappy uniform, sucking up to dickhead commuters day after day. He'd restore her to what she should be, his fucking old lady, sitting up on the back of the Yammy, spreading her arse across the back rest. He could feel

31

her tits pressing on his back and his arms straining with pride as he gripped the handlebars. Then he'd open his eyes and see the Goldie, immaculate but motionless, the grass growing up between her polished wheel spokes, the crutches lying like an accusation next to the oildrum, waiting.

The railway carriage, his home, battered and scraped, sat bereft of feminine touch, neither dirty nor clean. Behind the tatty curtains every surface was bestrewn with tools, dishes, everything left out within easy reach. He thought of Gloria's nice house, her little car. She probably had a nice little feller too; some twat in a suit, some clean and shiny wanker who worked in an estate agency or a building society – some fucker with two good legs.

It was futile but the dreams wouldn't go. He could change – for her. She wasn't meant for that humdrum life. Lots of guys rode bikes with damaged legs. He could get a trike, ride up to Piccadilly station, farting exhaust at all those fucking muppets in their cars and whisk her away.

He was cleaning the Goldie's crankcases when his ears picked up the sound, far away, like a warning of a swarm of bees, but it was so familiar to him. He was already indoors by the time the sound materialised into the low, throaty growls that told him these were no everyday bikes and he thanked God for the close spacing of his home, the single step between locking the carriage door and shutting himself in the tiny lavatory. He counted the different engine sounds as they slowed, circled, idled and stopped; listened as their voices started up, striving for recognition. Were they Outcasts? The sweat trickled down his neck. If only he could fucking see. They were next door, outside Gracelands.

'Hey man, what is this fucking place?'

'Fuck me, some biker lives here.'

They were rattling at the door, their heavy boots crunching the gravel, walking round the outside of the carriage. He could sense them peering through the windows. Jack held his breath, his back aching from holding himself still.

'No fucker at home,' someone said.

'Look at the Goldie. Looks like it's never moved in years.'

'Heap of shit.'

'Spotless shit though,' this last with grudging admiration.

'Some silly old cunt, too old to piss proper, dreaming about the war and all the tarts he shagged. Dreaming about doing a ton on some fucking old boneshaker.'

A rough voice cut across the laughter. 'Shut it man, you're not far off being an old cunt yourself. Have some fucking respect.'

'I don't fucking think so. Live fast – die young. Gorgon, you really going to buy this shithole?'

Jack closed his eyes. The walls closed in on him and the air seemed to turn fuzzy, as if it was being sucked from his body. It had come as he'd always known it would. Fucking Gorgon Garrett – so named after winning a cheese eating contest at the Nottingham Goose Fair rally. Not one of the Outcasts but one of the Hell Raiders, associates of the Outcasts in their drug dealing activities.

The two gangs hadn't always been on such good terms. Jack had been in the front line when years of bickering and skirmishes had come to a head in a final battle for supremacy out on Saddleworth Moor. The Outcasts had won. Jack had landed a bicycle chain across Gorgon's head, bringing him down so that Lenin could finish the job. There was no way Garrett would fail to recognise him.

Amazing what fear can do. How long did he stand there on his complaining legs, hardly breathing, barely thinking? He heard them tramp away and their voices died in the direction of the beach. He waited till they came back and invaded Gracelands. They were drinking and laughing outside. He could picture them sitting on their bikes, chaffing the young girls on their way from the caravan park to the amusement arcade. It seemed forever until he heard them getting ready to leave.

It wasn't until the noise of their engines had long died away and darkness fell and the sound of the karaoke starting up at the clubhouse brought normalcy back, that Jack came off the needle point of terror where he'd hung for the last four hours and knew what he had to do. What a fucking fool he'd been to think he could ever be safe. He'd had two and a half good years at Plotlands but that was an illusion.. Each time he heard or saw a bike, the memories, the terror swamped him. People talked – Rube in the café, Shazza with her fucking big mouth. It had only been a matter of time and now that cunt Gorgon Garrett would soon be on to him.

He'd been kidding himself about Gloria. There was no safety for her with him – being hunted down by the Outcasts. Once in, you could never really be out, even in exile and he still had something they wanted.

Garrett and his mob would be back and they would bring the Outcasts with them. No time like the fucking present. He went outside and looked at the Goldie. He could only take what he could carry on his back. Warm light washed across the road from Shazza's bungalow. To his left were the blank black windows of Gracelands and to his right the unfathomable dark where the road, civilisation and street lighting were swallowed up by the shore. Back inside, he retrieved his leather jacket from under his pillow, folding the colours to the inside, and stuffed it in the bottom of his rucksack.

Three Severed Feet

'Three you say?' Inspector Barnett pinched the space between his eyes where a headache was forming. It was four o'clock on Friday afternoon and he'd been looking forward to a quiet dinner with his wife in their local Italian restaurant with a bottle of Chianti to help him unwind. Now there was no chance.

'Exciting isn't it?' Chalmers said. He was avidly watching the continuing digging and the SOCO team moving round the derelict garden.

He was still young and curious, Inspector Barnett thought. 'Haven't you attended a murder scene before?' he asked.

'Of course,' Chalmers said, 'but well, y'know, three feet.'

'Any leads?' Barnett looked up from texting Margaret to say he didn't know when he'd get home.

'Nothing much so far. We may get a DNA match on the victims in time but we haven't found the rest of them yet.'

'Odd,' said Barnett stowing his phone. 'Do you think animals have been at them?'

'Can't tell yet. Some boys playing around in the empty gardens found them under those bushes at the far end.'

'Any idea how long they've been there?'

'Won't know accurately till later but I guess a good few weeks. They're pretty manky. Two of them have varnish on the toenails so probably a woman, though you can't tell these days.'

'No,' Barnett agreed. 'You talk to the boys?'

'Just kids on holiday at the caravan park; the family's from Ellesmere Port. They checked out okay, didn't know anything about the area. The house is empty, so's the one next door.'

'Who owns this dump I wonder.' Barnett eyed the faded sign that hung crookedly over the door of the dilapidated bungalow. 'Racelands – that's a funny name for a house. You talk to any of the neighbours?'

'No one seems to know much, seems the type of place where people keep themselves to themselves except there's a blonde woman across the way, gobby cow if you'll excuse me saying, Sir.'

'They're the best talkers,' Barnett gave a thin smile.

'Well she had plenty to say about the bloke who used to live here. She says he tried to kill her. I thought she was just a fantasist but when I checked the bloke's name, he'd been done for murdering his wife in Birkdale, near Southport years ago. Name of Graham Walters.

'Jesus,' said Barnett, 'what kind of people live here? Well, at least it looks like we'll be able to wrap this up once we know who the victims are.'

'It can't be him Sir, he's been dead nearly a year. Went into the quicksands on the beach here. Topped himself according to the woman over the road, Sharon Blake. Of course we can't be sure till after the p.m. but I'd lay odds those feet were walking around a few weeks ago.'

Barnett sighed. 'Why can't things be simple just for once?'

'She says the bloke next door did a runner a couple of months ago. No one knows where or why.'

'Suspicious,' Barnett said.

'And she clammed up when I started asking who owns the place now.'

'Did she?' Barnett said. 'I think we'd better pay her another visit.'

Got something to hide, Barnett thought as he stood on Sharon Blake's doorstep watching her eyes dart here and there behind her fringe of blonde hair.

'Could we come in for a moment?' he asked after introducing himself.

'Come in the kitchen.' She seemed flustered, closing the living room door as the two men filled the tiny hallway, but not before Barnett had seen the boxes of blag fags she had on her coffee table. He wasn't remotely interested in them but he would let her think he might be, to keep her off guard. He sat down at the kitchen table and looked pointedly at the kettle.

'Would you like a cuppa?' Sharon asked.

Before the kettle had even begun to boil she was spilling the beans about the former owner of the derelict chalet bungalow. If ever a woman could sing, it was this one, Barnett thought as she handed him his mug of tea.

He let her rattle on about how she'd practically been strangled. Personally he could quite understand how the poor bloke might have been driven to it. He lifted the mug to his lips. The tea was surprisingly good, strong and sweet as he liked it.

'But we really need to know about the last owner,' he said casually, keeping his eyes on his mug as he set it down. It bore a cartoon figure of a blonde ponytailed woman, not unlike Sharon and the words SEXY LADY blazoned across it in bright pink.

'The one you told me was buying the place,' Chalmers chipped in. His mug showed a large red heart and the words, I LUV SEX.

'I never knew his name,' Sharon cut him off. The smile slipped from her face.

'But you can describe him?'

'I don't remember.'

'I think you do,' Barnett said gently, 'it's very important you know.'

'Why?' Sharon said. 'What's going on?' She reached in her jeans pocket and pulled out a packet of Benson and Hedges. Barnett noticed that her hand was shaking.

'You've seen the men digging in the garden over there?'

Sharon nodded.

'We've found some human remains.'

'Oh my God!' The colour drained from her face leaving her looking aged and haggard. She fumbled a cigarette out of the packet. 'You don't mind do you?'

Barnett smiled and shook his head. 'It's your home,' he said. She'd obviously forgotten they were blags but he wasn't going to remind her.

'There was a whole gang of them,' she stuttered. 'They had stuff on their backs, like badges, denim waistcoat things over their leathers, with skulls and stuff on them.'

'Did you notice a name on them?' Chalmers asked.

Sharon sucked in smoke, held it. Her brow wrinkled. 'Hell something,' she said as she exhaled. 'Not Hell's Angels, Hell…'

'Raiders?' Chalmers supplied.

Sharon's face cleared then she looked at them warily and nodded. Both men sighed and sank back in their chairs like deflated footballs.

'They were going to buy it for a clubhouse, well the big one was.'

'Big one?' Barnett waited.

Sharon pulled on her cigarette, avoiding looking at the policemen.

'Black hair, bushy beard?' Barnett quizzed.

She was silent, then nodded slowly, her eyes still fixed on the table.

'You do know his name don't you?' Barnett pushed.

She looked uneasily round the room, dragged on her cigarette again. 'I don't know nothing,' she said. 'Why don't you leave me alone?'

'Someone's dead,' Chalmers said.

'Yeah and I don't wanna end up the same way,' Sharon snapped.

'Was it Pete?' Barnett asked quietly.

Sharon shifted in her seat. In the silence she seemed to shrink as the two men stared at her. At last she gave an imperceptible nod.

'Thank you,' Barnett said, 'that's a great help.' His face stayed impassive but his heart sank. Gorgon Garrett: he might have known he would be at the bottom of it somewhere. Chalmers looked at him enquiringly but said nothing in front of Sharon Blake. Barnett nodded gently to let him know the name meant something to him.

'The other man, the one who lived in the railway carriage, you say he disappeared?' Chalmers asked.

'Here one day and gone the next,' Sharon said. 'Never even said goodbye and the others never came back neither.' She seemed relieved that the

41

conversation was veering away from the Hell Raiders and much more willing to talk.

'What's his name, this man that lived in the railway carriage?' Chalmers persisted.

Sharon shrugged. 'Jack, that's all I ever knew,' she said. 'He left his bike behind when he went.' She puffed a cloud of cigarette smoke and squinted through it.

Barnett's stifled a cough and shifted to avoid the smoke. 'Another biker eh?'

'His bike's the last thing a biker would leave behind,' Chalmers said.

'Ex-biker.' Sharon stubbed her cig out in the ashtray on the table. 'It never moved all the time he was here. All he did was tinker with it, taking it to bits, cleaning it and all that. Don't think he could ride it, he had something wrong with his legs.'

'So what happened to it?' Barnett asked.

'Someone came and shifted it. He was only renting the place see. Someone came with a truck and stripped the place. That was about a month ago. No one's been back since.'

'Do you know who it was, who came and cleared the place out?' Chalmers flicked the pages of his notebook.

Sharon shook her head. 'I went across but they wouldn't talk to me. Two blokes, not bikers. They told me to mind my own business.'

'Any markings on the truck?'

'I don't think so. I don't remember.'

'Can you describe the men?'

'I don't really remember.'

'Did they go in the house?'

'No, they just picked up the bike and left.'

'What about the bungalow, Racelands?' Barnett said.

42

Sharon giggled. 'You mean Gracelands: someone who lived there ages ago used to be an Elvis freak. It's up for sale but I don't know who owns it. Like I told you, the bloke who lived there topped himself.'

Barnett turned to Chalmers. 'Once SOCO have finished, see if there's an estate agent's board anywhere. If not you can check all local agencies for both properties, we need to trace the owners. Ms Blake, we'll need to show you some photographs, see if you can identify the men who came in the truck.'

'It's a shame,' Sharon said. 'This place is going to rack and ruin. No one's going to want to live here now, finding bodies here.'

'Only feet so far,' Chalmers observed.

It didn't take long to trace the owner of Gracelands. It had belonged to Graham Walters but his disappearance into the quicksand appeared to have no relationship to the current murders. Whether his demise was accidental or deliberate was of no real interest to Barnett. The property had passed to his middle-aged sister who had promptly put it in the hands of a Rhyl estate agent but no prospective buyers had materialised until Peter Garrett had come along.

'Pity it fell through,' the receptionist told Chalmers, 'he seemed really keen. It would make an ideal holiday home.'

Chalmers thought about the dilapidated Gracelands and wondered if estate agencies trained all their staff in optimism. 'Did he say why he wasn't buying it?' he enquired.

'We never heard from him again after the viewing,' she said, scrolling down her computer screen.

'Were you aware that the lock on the back door had been forced?'

'Not until the police told us. We've secured it temporarily now it's been released.'

Luckily for Chalmers the same office handled the letting of the railway carriage next door to Gracelands which belonged to a North West property company and had been rented out to Jack Philips on an annual lease. He'd been there two and a half years.

'Do you know exactly when he left?'

'Well, no, only that his rent stopped coming in two months ago and when the owners sent someone round the place was empty. Apparently he left a lot of stuff behind. It's still vacant.' The receptionist pulled a printed detail sheet from her desk drawer. Chalmers studied it, noting the same optimism in the property's description as 'a quaint and characterful dwelling place.'

'Someone went round and cleared out his possessions, was that done through your agency?'

'No, we wouldn't do that. Probably the property company or even the tenant himself, after all he never returned the keys.'

'Not a lot to go on,' Chalmers told Barnett. 'Sharon Blake couldn't or wouldn't identify anyone from the mugshots. Jack Philips has a record, minor stuff mostly, theft, burglary, assault. He used to run with a bike gang but there's nothing recent. He seems to have disappeared off the map a couple of years ago.'

'Running from something,' Barnett mused. 'Maybe it caught up with him. Did you find out which outfit he was with?'

'The Outcasts,' Chalmers referred to his notes.

'Garrett is with the Hell Raiders,' Barnett made a moue of disgust. 'There's an uneasy truce between the two gangs – at least where their criminal activities are concerned.'

'I couldn't find anything on Garrett.'

'No, you won't. He's a slippery bastard. Never actually been done for anything, yet we know he's been behind some major robberies and more than one murder. Some other sucker usually carries the can. I've locked horns with him once or twice in the past. Nasty piece of work.'

'You think he came after Philips?'

'Tempting,' Barnett sucked his teeth, 'but we can't jump to conclusions. The pathologist says the two female feet belong to one person, probably late twenties.'

'Any ideas?' Chalmers asked.

'Garrett has a girlfriend, Roxanne Parker, lives in Birkenhead. We'd better look her up. The other foot's male, 30-35 in age. Could fit Philips, he's thirty-six. No sign of the rest of the bodies, even though both gardens have been combed. The murders took place in the living room of Gracelands. Massive bloodstains on the carpets, no attempt to clean them up.'

'Strange.' Chalmers shook his head.

Roxanne Parker was missing from home, well, not exactly missing. She'd gone off three months earlier with Garrett, as far as her family knew. Apparently they were accustomed to her absences so they hadn't reported her missing.

'Gone off and left her kid for us mugginses to look after,' her father told Chalmers on the doorstep, indicating a small girl clinging to his leg. 'Hasn't even been in touch or sent any money for the baby.'

'Is that usual?' Chalmers asked

'It's not unusual. You never know with our Josie.'

'Josie?'

'Roxy's the name she took up once she got in with them bikers,' the father explained. 'Josie's not good enough for her I suppose.'

'Is she in the habit of wearing nail varnish?'

'I dunno. I suppose so, not summat I'd take much notice of. You better come in and ask the wife.'

Barnett lay in the single bed in the spare room where he always slept if he came home after midnight in order not to disturb Margaret. Sleepless in the small hours, he pondered the possibilities of the severed feet.

Chalmers had persuaded Roxanne Parker's parents to give up a hairbrush for DNA testing so hopefully they should have a result fairly soon. He was fairly sure the female feet belonged to Parker but what about the male one? If they could find the rest of the bodies it would be easy to identify Garrett by the tattoo of a python that ran all down the left side of his body.

Obviously Jack Philips had been hiding out from someone. Maybe Garrett had come looking for him and Philips had killed him. But then why the female feet? Garrett wouldn't come on a revenge mission with his girlfriend? It must have been an accidental meeting, just a coincidence that Garrett had thought of buying the house next door. It made sense that he would bring Roxanne Parker to look at the place with him. Yet Philips seemed an unlikely murderer, after all, he'd run away to hide from something. By all accounts he was at

46

least partly disabled and a loner. How could he have disposed of the bodies?

No, it was much more likely that Garrett was the perpetrator and the male foot belonged to Philips. But then what was the motive for killing Parker as well? Unless the feet weren't Parker's, maybe belonged to a girlfriend of Philips.

'The DNA matches. The feet are Parker's.' Chalmers announced.

'And no sign of Garrett?' Barnett sat back from his computer.

'No sign of any of the Hell Raiders,' Chalmers said. 'They seem to have disappeared off the face of the earth.'

'That's suspicious in itself.' Barnett swivelled to and fro on his chair.

'So what are you thinking, Boss?'

'I think Philips was having it off with Roxanne Parker. You know what these bikers are like; they fight over anything, it's all pride with them. I think Garrett found out where Philips lived and bumped him off and her as well.'

'So where are the bodies – and why the feet?'

'My guess is they're in the quicksand but I have to admit the feet have got me stumped.'

'Very funny Sir,' Chalmers allowed himself a small smile.

Just then the phone rang and Chalmers listened as his boss whistled in response to what he was being told.

'Right then,' Barnett slammed the receiver down. 'Come on. We're going out.'

They both stared at the blackened foot lying on the table. A lab assistant was carefully cleaning it.

'Where was it?' Barnett asked.

'Someone's dog fetched it home. Looks like it was buried in sand.'

Chalmers checked his notebook. 'Name of Rajah – the dog Sir, not the owner. His name is Bill Wicklow, he's a local pensioner.'

Something was emerging on the rotting skin as the sand was cleaned away.

'Looks like a tree root,' Chalmers said.

'Or the tail of a snake,' Barnett said.

'Garrett,' Chalmers said.

Barnett sucked his teeth. 'I want Jack Philips found. You'd better get on it right away.'

'One of the Outcasts till a couple of years ago,' Chalmers said. 'There was a row over some woman. He ended up in hospital. He's practically a cripple now; even that woman Blake says so. I can't see him chopping anyone's feet off.'

'Why would anyone want to do that anyway?' Barnett mused.

'Philips's fingerprints are all over the crime scene,' Chalmers said, 'but then they would be. Apparently he was pally with the bloke who used to live there.'

'None in the blood, I don't suppose?'

'No, but I've just got some results. There was a bloody fingerprint found on the kitchen tap. It belongs to Wayne Johnson, runs with the Outcasts. He's got a record a mile long, sadistic bastard from what I hear. Goes by the name of Hannibal.'

'Just a minute.' Barnett sat down and feverishly clicked his computer keyboard. 'You contacted the owner of Dunroamin yet?'

'It's a property company,' Chalmers said. 'I haven't been able to make contact yet. No one's answering the phone or email.'

'Ah.' Barnett stabbed the scroll key triumphantly. 'Here we are. Homesearch Properties.'
Chalmers bent to look where he was pointing. 'Director, Wayne Johnson.'

Barnett got to his feet. 'Let's have him in.'

Hannibal was something of a misnomer, Barnett thought, surveying the weedy specimen across the desk but then he saw the flint-mean streak in the man's eyes and began to revise his opinion. He'd brushed with the Outcasts before and remembered their former leader Jeffrey Armstrong aka Lenin. He'd been a skinny runt too but hard, Barnett had to admit that.

'I don't know where the fucker went,' Johnson replied when asked about his former tenant. 'Wish I did – he owes me two months' rent.'

'How long had he been your tenant?' Chalmers asked.

'Fucked if I remember. Never met the cunt. Didn't even know his name. All done through the estate agent.'

'Someone cleared the property after he left. Did you organise that?'

'Don't know nothing about that. Cheeky fucker must have come back and done it; he's still got my keys.'

Barnett regarded Johnson in silence. The biker's filthy jeans were full of holes revealing patches of skin stained with dirty engine oil and his grimy hands showed black-rimmed fingernails as he toyed nervously with a rollup cigarette.

'How did you come to own the place,' he glanced at his screen, 'Dunroamin?'

'Bought it as an investment. Thought it might make a sort of clubhouse but we never used it so I decided to let it out.'

'You have other 'investments'?' Chalmers asked. 'Homesearch Properties? Quite the businessman aren't you?'

Johnson shrugged, leaned back in his seat and gave Chalmers a mean stare.

Barnett took the lead. 'Of course you knew your tenant was a former member of the Outcasts – Jack Philips?'

Johnson jerked forward. 'Bollocks!' he spat, his narrowed eyes fixed on Barnett's face.

'He was hiding from someone?' Barnett dropped the question while the man's guard was down.

A shutter seemed to close behind Johnson's eyes. 'I don't know nothing about it,' he muttered.

'What about Peter Garrett – Gorgon?' Chalmers said, taking the hint as Barnett glanced at him.

Johnson stared at him.

'He was buying the place next door, Gracelands.'

'So?'

'You were pally with him weren't you? Outcasts and Hell Raiders do business together?'

Johnson shifted in his seat. 'What's this all about anyway?'

Barnett leaned forward, let menace seep into his voice. 'You know damned well. Two people were killed in that dump next door to your property. The floor was covered in blood. We found body parts in the garden.'

'I don't know what you're on about,' Johnson leaned back in his seat again.

'One of them was Roxanne Parker.'

'Roxy? You don't say?'

'The other was Gorgon Garrett. Don't play the innocent with me. What did you do with the rest of the bodies?'

'You got the wrong bloke,' Johnson said, 'think again.'

'You were there,' Barnett said quietly.

'Who says so? I was at my girlfriend's house. Ask her.'

'Oh, none of your mates have talked,' Barnett said. He left a silence, watching as Johnson's brow furrowed slightly. 'The evidence did,' he finally said.

'What evidence? You got nothing on me.' Johnson struggled to sound cocky.

'A fingerprint,' Chalmers said. 'Your fingerprint – at the crime scene.'

'So what? I been there a few weeks ago, there was a party, Gorgon was looking the place over.'

'A bloody fingerprint,' Barnett said, 'on the kitchen tap, where you washed your hands afterwards.'

Johnson kept his face immobile but Barnett saw sweat break out on his forehead.

'You buried them in the quicksand and I expect the murder weapons too, but you dropped the feet – or someone else did. You didn't do this on your own.'

'Prove it.'

'Oh we will,' Barnett said. 'Tell us who was with you, it might go easier for you.'

'Fuck you,' Johnson said.

'What was it, a fight over the woman – or money, or drugs?'

'No comment,' Johnson said, 'I want my brief.'

'Happy to oblige,' Barnett smiled. 'Just tell me one thing. Why the feet? Why did you cut off their feet? We know they were still alive when you did it.'

An evil grin spread over Johnson's face turning it into a devilish mask that Barnett knew would haunt his dreams for a long time to come.

'So they couldn't run away,' Johnson said and snickered.

Transplanted Heart

The tomatoes were beyond redemption, sandblasted in Saturday night's storm. Bill looked at them in despair. Even now on Monday morning, the wind whipped sharply in from the Plotlands beach, scouring his face with invisible grains.

He bent to the soil, scooped some in his hand and rubbed it through his fingers, feeling the grit of sand and silica sifting back to earth. Useless. In his mind he saw himself testing the black peaty soil of the farm, squeezing its moisture against his palm, knowing that it was just right. He remembered the sharp smell of the young cabbages, bunched ready for planting and the soft dampness of the West Lancashire air where rain was never far away. He put out his tongue to taste it and instead caught the tang of the sea, the dry gust of the July heat and he opened his eyes. Instead of his flat acres of carrots and potatoes, the creeping morning mists blurring the edges of the land, he saw the ice-cream parlour across the road and a family of holidaymakers in shorts and tee shirts, the children with balls and buckets and spades, sitting outside on the wooden bench and staring at him.

He looked down at his feet where Lacie's 'Fairy' rose bloomed vigorously against the dying tomato vines. It thrived there, like Lacie herself, who fitted in so well with the bingo sessions, the Tuesday craft group and the monthly tea dances.

'Stop daydreaming and get your coat on. Janie'll have dinner on the table.' Lacie had come into the garden without him noticing her.

Who needed a coat in this heat? Still, he let her fuss him into a light jacket because he was busy looking in the lines of her face for the young girl full of energy she'd once been. It was the way he kept thinking of her lately, remembering how she'd shared a tumbledown cottage with him without complaint, before Dad died and his mother had turned the farm over to him.

Rajah was in his basket by the fireplace even though the gas fire wasn't turned on. Was he too dreaming of the old days, drying out in front of the kitchen range after a winter's day in the rain-sodden fields?

On the short drive to Prestatyn, Bill's thoughts turned to Janie as they got nearer to her home. Janie and the kids were the future and when he pulled up in the street and Ceri came toddling down the path with Ieuan running behind, the past fell away and ceased to plague him for a while.

'At least your mum taught you how to cook properly,' he said, mopping the last of the lamb stew from his plate with a bit of bread.

'Good Welsh lamb,' Janie grinned. She leaned forward to wipe gravy from Ceri's chin. Bill looked at the baby; saw first Janie, then himself and his mother peeping out from the child's features. The little boy, Ieuan, looked more like his father, a rough shepherd kind of look, despite the soft curves of his face. Did David have sheep farming ancestors? Bill didn't think so, with his love of engines and their inner workings. Bill knew how to chivvy a tractor all right but the intricacies of spark plugs, rods and pistons, the smells of grease and diesel, held no attraction for him.

'Not Ormskirk tatties though,' Lacie said and Bill smiled to himself.

'Why didn't you bring Rajah, Grampy?' Ieuan asked.

'Rajah gets tired,' Janie said. 'He's getting old now. You can see him on Sunday at Nanny and Gramps's house.'

'Can we go to the beach?' Ieuan tugged at Bill's sleeve, 'and have ice cream?'

'Ith cream,' Ceri shouted and banged her spoon on the tray of her high chair.

'Come for tea,' Lacie said, 'we can all go to the club after.'

Bill smothered a groan.

'You needn't look like that,' Lacie said.

'Karaoke? No thanks.'

'You don't have to come.' Her voice was tart. 'Stay at home with your precious tomatoes.'

'You should get out more, socialise,' Janie said. She put her elbows on the table, leaned her chin on her hands. Bill thought of her, aged ten, engrossed in a storybook, the sunlight streaming round her as she curled on her bedroom window seat. 'You've been here a year now and you haven't made a single friend.'

He never had been one for friends. He'd been too busy working the land. Lacie was his friend, she'd always been enough. Oh, he'd been in the company of other farmers at NFU get togethers, auction sales and the like but he'd never been one for boozing and boasting. When he'd been a lad the farm used to teem with folk. He hadn't realised how solitary he'd become as agriculture dwindled and mechanised.

Anyway, it wasn't true. He'd got quite friendly with that chap with the motorbike, Jack till he disappeared one day. No one knew where he'd gone and Bill wasn't

55

one for gossip but he often wondered where he was when he passed the closed up railway carriage. The one next to it was empty too, it's for sale sign already bleached by the weather. Milly Pink had said some other biker was going to buy it and Bill hadn't liked the sound of that. And then there'd been that terrible day when Rajah'd picked that thing up, the thing he'd thought was an old bone. Who'd have thought it, murders in a place like Plotlands. Understandable that the house was still empty; who would want to live there? Unbelievably he bloke who'd lived there before had been a murderer too, so Lacie said, but she'd got that from Milly Pink so Bill took it with a pinch of salt.

Milly Pink was one for tales and tattle but he didn't take her on. Still, he was friendly enough to her, always said a few words when he went in for his paper. He didn't care for the people in the next bungalow, retired townies – and they were only there odd weekends and for a few weeks in the summer.

'You should try some of the activities at the community centre, like Mum.'

'What – sequence dancing and bingo?'

'There are things for men too – bowls, chess.'

Bill snorted. He didn't want to admit he hadn't a clue how to play chess but even if there were darts and dominoes, he wasn't interested.

'You could start a gardening club.'

'Growing what – marram grass and dog roses?'

'Don't be so defeatist.' Janie stood up and began gathering the plates together.

She didn't understand. What could he say to these people who knew nothing of who he was, how all his knowledge was in his fingertips, in the felt water content of a leaf, in the density of a stem? It was in his nose: the sting of electricity in the air when a storm was coming, the first scent of pollen releasing from a newly budded field of rape. These folk he lived among barely knew an apple from an onion. They talked about television programmes and football scores.

Janie picked Ceri from her high chair and handed her to Lacie. Bill watched her bounce the giggling baby, her face crinkling up in a smile. Ieuan got down from the table and began to play with a toy garage and a box of cars on the floor.

'Mark phoned last night,' Janie said over her shoulder as she took the plates into the kitchen. 'He's been promoted to store manager.'

'Hmph,' said Bill. Mark made him feel prickly as a thistle. He should have taken on the farm, not gone pussyfooting about working in shops. What kind of life was that for a farmer's son? He didn't blame Janie for not staying on the farm. It wasn't a job for a single woman. It hadn't hurt too much when she'd met David while working at the holiday camp because he'd expected Mark to take over the farm, but Mark had let him down.

His blood still ran hot when he thought about it. All those years of bringing him up, teaching him the business of the farm. He'd set him small tasks when he was little: picking the new potatoes and peas, looking after the chickens, helping with the kitchen garden. He'd done it carefully, feeding him responsibility as the boy grew. By the time he was twelve he could work like a man, driving the tractor and drowning the feral kittens from the barn without a qualm. 'My lad,' he used to think, watching him go about his chores after school.

It had all been so natural, so taken for granted that as Bill's strength waned, Mark would take over stewardship of the land. Then to turn round at sixteen and say, 'Sorry Dad, it's not going to happen, I don't want to be a farmer.' He'd almost staggered from the blow.

Mark had just shrugged. 'There's no future in farming,' and his face had closed up against every argument and threat Bill threw at him. Something changed then in the way Bill looked at his son, as if he wasn't part of the family at all. He'd come round in the end, accepted Mark's desertion, made an uneasy peace but when they met, he always felt awkward, had nothing now to say to him.

'It's a big step up for him,' Janie called from the sink

Bill grunted but he couldn't help feeling a sneaking pride – his son running a great place like that, in charge of all those people and all that food from all over the world. But still, it wasn't right. If it hadn't been for Mark, he and Lacie would still have been at the farm, enjoying their retirement in their rightful place.

Janie returned with mugs of tea. 'Come on Dad, you should be pleased for him. Every little helps.' She grinned as she passed him the sugar.

'Didn't help us,' he muttered.

'It wasn't Mark's fault the land got bought up.'

Bill thought about the great warehouse that now covered his five-acre field, the access road and mini-roundabout fronting the farmhouse that still stood there, a monument to his life and the generations of his family. Probably turned into offices now, or rented out to some commuter who couldn't care less about it. Damned councils, damned conglomerates. It made him boil to think about it.

'Anyway,' Janie said, 'you'd have had to retire in the end. You couldn't have kept on working the farm.'

He was speechless with temper, daren't open his mouth. He was seventy two, not ninety, and as strong as he'd always been. He forced himself to concentrate on Lacie, on how happy she was, close to her child, her grandchildren. If she could settle for this, why couldn't he?

Back at Plotlands, he whistled Rajah and put the German Shepherd on his lead.

'Just going for the Guardian, want anything from the shop?'

'Pick up some milk; I'll put the kettle on.' Lacie was getting out her knitting. He knew her mind was already on the afternoon TV quiz shows.

The beach road was crowded, the small public car park packed. There would be no peace now till the school holidays ended if this weather kept up. He matched his pace to Rajah's. The dog was getting slow. They ambled past the tinny noise of the amusement arcade and turned left by the Pirates' Inn to Milly Pink's shop. Rajah stood patiently beside him as he waited while Milly doled out sweets, drinks and ice lollies to the queue in front. At last his turn came and Milly reached under the counter for his weekly treat.

'Farmers' Guardian?'

He nodded.

'How's Lacie? Coming to the pub quiz tonight?'

'I expect so. Her's fine.'

'Tell her I'll see her there then.'

'Okay.'

He went the long way back along the nature walk through the dunes, letting Rajah off his lead. The dog could still run, snuffling off across the close turf after the smells of rabbits but he would never catch one now. Bill was tempted to sit down on the bench looking out over the muddy sands to read his paper. He itched to open it, plunge back into the world of potato prices, wheat and barley yields. Instead, he tucked the paper under his arm, savouring the prospect of sitting in the garden to read it with a cup of tea and a slice of Lacie's lemon cake. He skirted the artificial ponds, created as a habitat for the natterjack toads that had been introduced around the same time he and Lacie had moved there, and looked askance at the plantings of honeysuckle and dog roses. 'Bloody nonsense, putting things where they don't belong,' he thought, whistling Rajah as he made his way home.

In the garden he moved his chair to a shady spot under the scrawny silver birch and turned his back to the house and the remains of the tomatoes. He turned the pages of the Guardian with ceremony, looking for familiar names or places, when an advert caught his eye.

Experienced agricultural worker wanted for large mixed arable farm. Cottage available.

It was meant for him. Delicious joy crept through him. Arable had been his whole life. If anyone had experience it was him – fifty years of it. You're too old, a voice said in his head and he was back at Janie's, burning with shame and anger as she told him he couldn't have gone on.

'Rubbish!' he said out loud. He was fit, his body strong as ever despite how Lacie fussed over him. He looked at the address. Lydiate, Merseyside – almost home. Back in his own landscape, a small speck against a sky that went on forever, instead of being hemmed in by these higgledy-piggledy Welsh hills.

He was hot with excitement, wanted to rush in and tell Lacie but at the thought of her a chill set in. She

60

would never go for it – but if he went after it, if he got the job, surely then she wouldn't refuse? – and there was a cottage too. It wasn't so far away…

The introductory music to *Deal or No Deal* drifted from the open back door, mingling with the faint music of the arcade. Bill stared at the paper but saw nothing, his mind full of the future, life on a new farm, all the pleasure of the work he loved but none of the responsibility. Rajah slept at his feet and as the sun slanted and dipped the garden deeper in shade, his head nodded and the mumbling of bees in Lacie's roses smoothed his thoughts into dreams.

When he awoke, Lacie was calling him for his tea and he knew there was something important he had to do but he couldn't remember what it was until he folded his paper. He held the secret inside himself through the meal. He would make the phone call later, when Lacie had gone to the club and there was no chance of being disturbed.

'Milly said she'd see you at the quiz,' he said and was pleased when she nodded. She knew better than to ask him to accompany her.

In the morning he woke early with a sense of loss, of something undone – and then he remembered. Why hadn't he made that phone call? He'd started to punch in the number half a dozen times but that image of Janie kept stopping him; that sympathetic pitying look that said he was past it.

Lacie was still asleep. Last night he'd been afraid of what she might say but now with the energetic morning sun shafting through a gap in the curtains, it all looked different. He would get up, go down and make that call but still a faint sense of unease clung to him as he quietly slipped on his clothes and crept downstairs.

Rajah was not in his basket. He lay on the rug by the back door, his eyes half-open. One touch told Bill he was dead. He staggered under the weight of the dog's body as he lifted him. Outside, he fetched his spade from the shed, scraped a hole in the poor sandy soil. Rajah was a big dog and Bill was out of breath by the time he'd finished.

Only the birds sang. Plotlands was silent and empty at this hour. Bill looked back at the house. No point in waking Lacie yet. The sun was fully up now, harsh and bright but a chill still sharpened the air. Bill took his jacket from the hook by the back door and walked up the empty beach road to the nature reserve. Rajah's lead was still in his pocket. He passed the artificial ponds. There was no sign of the natterjack toads.

Since Janine Left

Petra never answers back. She doesn't nag or ask awkward questions. Lee likes that. It's been quiet at The Haven since Janine left.

It never would have worked for him and Janine. He should have known someone who designed embroidery kits for a living would not be the passionate fireball he really wanted. Not like Petra sitting there on the sofa now with her legs crossed, giving him a discreet flash of her panties, a promise of what was to come later.

No, he should never have got married to Janine but then it hadn't just been for the sex that soon dwindled to hardly ever. It had also been for love. He'd been an only child, sent to a boys' school and girls had been an alien race to him. He'd always been mad on computers and when he did start to get interested in girls he was awkward and always felt they were laughing at him. He retreated more and more into his virtual world as he went into adulthood.

So it was always difficult, meeting women, talking to them but then he'd designed Janine's website. She'd been one of his first customers, when he was still advertising in the newsagent's window near his mother's home in Radcliffe. Somehow romance had developed through the emails and phone calls so that when they did actually meet it was easier, even though she was a bit older than him at thirty-two.

Lee sighs, looks at his reflection in the living room mirror. Women have called him ugly – is that a bad thing in a man? No matter how often he washes it, his hair always looks greasy. He fetches the brush from the sideboard, takes Petra's long blonde hair out of its ponytail and starts to brush, feeling her relax under his fingers, although she doesn't take her eyes off Eastenders.

The long rhythmic strokes give him pleasure. Janine's hair was too short for brushing, short as her temper became after they moved to Plotlands. It had been her idea, the move: somewhere quiet where they could take long walks along the beach or through the dunes to Gronant; somewhere they could concentrate on their work and on loving each other. Janine's embroidery designs quite often featured romantic princes and princesses. Lee thinks how she probably never really saw him as he was. He glances at himself again in the mirror. Frog Prince. He pulls a face and smiles because it doesn't matter any more.

Petra smiles too. Her legs have splayed further open and her skirt has ridden up. She doesn't push it down. The hair brushing makes Lee horny. He undoes the top button on Petra's silk blouse and slips a finger inside.

'Time for bed, baby?' he whispers in her ear and feels her melt against him in a way Janine rarely did. The approach to sex with Janine was always fraught with courtship rituals, even after they married. Always having to try so hard made him feel unworthy.

In the bedroom he undresses Petra carefully and picks out the black baby doll pyjamas, genuine vintage, that he bought her on eBay. He likes to spend money on her clothes and makeup. After all, she's a lot less expensive than Janine, doesn't make constant demands for holidays and restaurant meals.

He cleans off her makeup with Johnson's baby lotion and cotton wool. He loves to see her all made up

64

but he loves the routine of cleansing too, seeing her skin smooth and pink and naked.

Her breasts gleam through the black nylon of her pyjama top. He rubs a hand over them, enjoying the silky feel of the fabric and the weight of her flesh. He specifically asked for large breasts. She'd cost more than the standard model but she was worth it. The price had staggered him when he'd first come across the Unconditional Love website but there were few running costs. Not that he would stint her; she's too good for that.

Petra came with three tongues. He keeps them in a box by the bedside. Now he takes it out and selects the long, soft one. 'Treat for you tonight,' he whispers as he changes the tongue and tucks her into bed. He sings 'Love me tender,' as he washes the daytime tongue in the bathroom and returns it to the box before he slips into bed, feeling Petra's familiar curves press against him as he reaches for the baby oil on the bedside cabinet.

Something is wrong with Petra. She lolls on the sofa in unladylike poses. No matter how carefully Lee sits her down, her arms flop and flap, she won't hug or comfort him. It is like Janine all over again except that this time he knows she doesn't mean it. He rings the Unconditional Love helpline. They tell him it's a common problem, easily fixed, nothing to worry about. He feels reassured.

Two service engineers arrive promptly but he doesn't like the way they examine Petra, putting their hands all over her under her clothes, pulling her arms and legs.

'Happens all the time,' says the ginger-haired one. 'Joints go loose with use, see?'

Lee blushes. He stares at them both but their faces are perfectly straight.

'She'll have to go back to the service centre,' the fair one says.

'How long for?' Anxiety strains through his voice.

'Week, two weeks.' Ginger shrugs. 'Specialist job, see? And there's a backlog at the moment.'

'Noooo,' Lee wails. How will he manage without her? The engineers stare at him in surprise. 'It's just that….' He dries up, knowing they don't understand. He fusses as they pack her into her original box and carry her out to their van. It reminds him of when his aunty Meg died and he has to keep telling himself that she will soon come back but he is so afraid he will never see her again. He wants to kiss her goodbye but he can't in front of the two men.

'Someone'll ring you when she's ready, mate.' They jump in the van and drive away. Lee wonders if they are laughing about him.

He misses her more than he thought possible. Four days pass, the house is empty and his bed is cold. He tries to lose himself in his work and manages it for a few hours each day till eyestrain makes him stop and her absence presses in once more. It is almost as bad as when Janine left but at least this time he knows Petra will come back.

When it gets unbearable, he walks along the top path to the lighthouse, or up to the ruined abbey on the hill across the road from Plotlands. Occasionally he plays around on Facebook but mostly only to gain contacts for work. He's never been a sociable person, not one for going out or joining things. He's been in Plotlands nearly two years now and barely speaks to anyone, only Milly Pink, when he has to go in her shop for something.

On the fourth night he dreams Petra is in bed beside him, her body fitted round him. He is about to enter her when something in the depths of her eyes stops him. Her lips open.

'Lee baby, I'm sorry,' she says gently. 'This just isn't working.'

He jerks back, a sweat of fear bursting from his pores, then seizes her chin, searches her eyes, sees they are Janine's eyes; it is Janine pulling away from him. He wakes, sweat sheening his body, fumbling the empty space where his woman should be until relief rights the panic inside him. He clutches the pillow realising for the first time how similar Petra's features are to Janine's. Only their hair is different. He has had this dream before, the trace memory of Janine's departure, replayed in different ways only with all the same pain. It will never happen to him again, not with Petra.

When the doorbell rings on the fifth day his heart jumps, thinking they have brought Petra back. Maybe he was out when they rang, or maybe they just didn't bother.

There's a blonde on the doorstep, thirty-something, Lee guesses, with big breasts. They're peeping out of her top, although the summer breeze is chilly. Apart from the breasts, she's not his type, tight lycra pants and cheap trainers. But her hair is long and blonde, tied up the way he ties up Petra's and this attracts him. There the resemblance ends. This woman's hair is coarse and badly bleached; her face is red and blotchy.

She smells of cigarettes. He thinks of the delicate perfume Janine always wore: the same one he now buys for Petra – 'Je Reviens' – ironic really.

He realises she is waiting for him to speak. 'Yes?' he says, noticing the bundle of flyers in her hand. He knows her by sight; he's seen her around and in the shop. She lives near the bus stop in a rundown prefab.

'Er – I'm just coming round looking for work.' She shifts her chewing gum from one cheek to the other. 'I run a cleaning business. I'm local you know, my name's Sharon but everyone calls me Shazza.'

'No thanks.' He moves to close the door but her foot is in the way.

'Looks like you could do with it.' She nods at The Haven's dilapidated porch. 'I've seen you around. Been on your own for a while haven't you? If you don't mind me saying.'

Lee does mind but he takes the flyer from her. Nosy bitch, he thinks, they don't miss a trick round here. He's heard them nattering in Milly Pink's shop about people he doesn't know. Do they talk about him too?

When she's gone, he looks round The Haven, sees it how other people might look at it. He rarely tidies up nowadays. It doesn't seem to matter much and it's one thing Petra can't do. Maybe it wouldn't hurt to get the woman in to give the place a good going over. Janine would be horrified if she saw it now. Women like things to look nice. It will be a surprise for Petra when she comes back.

'What happened to your wife, then?' Shazza asks him on her third visit, over coffee. He's already got used to her straight-out way of talking.

68

'It just didn't work out. Specially after we moved here. We weren't really suited, I suppose.'

'No chance of you getting back together again?'

'No. We've been divorced six months now.'

'Seems a shame, you here all on your own.' She smiles at him, he thinks with sympathy, not pity or curiosity. He wants to tell her that he's not alone but he knows that Petra is best kept secret.

'I'm going outside for a cig,' she says, getting up and giving him an eyeful of her cleavage. 'Then I'll give the bedroom a good hoovering.'

Luckily the wardrobe has a key and the key is in Lee's pocket. He doesn't want Shazza pawing through Petra's things and asking questions. He puts the baby oil and the box of tongues in the wardrobe together with Petra's makeup. It feels like he is putting Petra out of his life but it's only temporary, until she comes back. When Janine walked out she didn't left much behind but it was ages before he could part with the few items: her old toothbrush, a dog-eared pair of slippers, a few books. It was only after Petra had settled in that he felt able to put them in the wheelie bin. He gave the books to Milly Pink for the second-hand bookshelf in her shop. Shazza doesn't ask about the locked wardrobe. She knows certain places are out of bounds, like the tiny dining room that is now Lee's workplace-cum-study.

He has to admit that The Haven is a different place since Shazza's been coming. It's nice to have things clean and in places where he can find them and he likes to see the sun shining through the windows. He watches the movement of Shazza's hips as she sweeps the hoover back and forth. When she invites him to the cabaret night at the community club, he doesn't refuse.

On the fifteenth day of Petra's absence, the phone rings while Lee is relaxing on his bed. Shazza has allowed him to rub his penis between her breasts and now his head is empty as he watches her hanging out his freshly washed curtains in the garden.

'Who? What?' It takes him some time to realise who is calling him and to understand the message. Petra is ready to come home. 'Today? No. No, you can't. I'm busy. I have an appointment. Tomorrow, it'll have to be tomorrow.' Tomorrow Shazza doesn't come round. It's Thursday, the day she goes on the bus to Rhyl to do her shopping. They have a date for the evening but he'll have to put her off. He can't leave Petra alone on her first night back, can he?

Now he will have to get rid of Shazza, tell her he doesn't need her any more but when she comes back in, smelling of clean linen, and presses herself against him, turning her face up to be kissed, he realises that he does need her, a real, warm woman.

'What's the matter, lover boy?' She puts a hand up to his crinkled forehead. All the post-orgasm sleepiness has gone from him; he's as tense as a prizefighter entering the ring.

'I had a phone call. Urgent job. It means I can't make our date tomorrow.'

She pouts. 'I was going to cook your favourite curry.'

'I'm sorry. Let's make it Friday instead.'

'That's my line dancing night.' She frowns.

'Tell you what, I'll take you out for a meal, somewhere nice – how about the Riverside?'

She's pleased. The Riverside is posh. She goes off happy, leaving Lee to wrestle with the problem of keeping two women. It doesn't occur to him to get rid of Petra. She's been in his life too long and she gives him everything he wants. She is so special to him and so – faultless. On the other hand he's starting to have feelings for Shazza despite her chewing gum, her cigs and her bossy ways. But real women are unpredictable, look what happened with Janine.

Petra doesn't complain about staying in the study in the day. She takes her rightful place in the evenings when Lee isn't seeing Shazza, and at nights in their bed. Then he can show her how happy he is to have her back and he can tell she is just as happy to be home, even though Shazza rules in the day.

Their sex life is even better now, not just because Petra is stronger and more flexible after her servicing but because Lee feels so much more amorous, going from one woman to the other. It turns him on, being so desirable. He is so happy with this situation that he wants it to go on forever. Sometimes he wonders which one he loves the most but love is an emotion he shies away from since Janine left. When he thinks like this the concept of choice rears: the suggestion that one day he will have to choose and he pushes these ideas away. It is an area of thought as dodgy as the Plotlands quicksands.

'Coffee's ready.' Shazza rattles the knob on the study door.

'Coming.' He opens it just a crack, so she can't see Petra lounging on the daybed he keeps in there. She's wearing her pink microskirt and her knees are tucked up under her chin so her matching panties are on show.

She's got that innocent but lascivious look on her face with her tongue just visible between her teeth.

'Come on, you've been in there for hours.' Shazza is starting to take over the house now: setting up timetables for lunch and coffee, suggesting buying new lamps and curtains. 'What have you got in there anyway that's so secret? Dead bodies?'

He's too shocked to laugh. 'It's just my work,' he mutters. 'I don't want things moved.'

'Bet you're a regular Bluebeard.' She stops mid-laugh and a curious look passes over her face but it's gone in a moment when he suggests a trip to Warrington to visit Ikea.

He thinks he will have to be more careful. She has a key to the front door now so that he doesn't have to stay in all the time when she comes to clean. Sometimes he needs to be alone. He keeps the study door locked, the key clanking against the wardrobe key in his trouser pocket as he walks. At times he fantasises that Shazza finds Petra and accepts her. In these daydreams they live happily together, all three of them pleasuring and loving each other.

So does he decide to do it unconsciously – the day he goes into Rhyl to meet a client and forgets to lock the study door? The client, Ella Jacobs, is a middle-aged woman setting up an holistic therapy business for survivors of abuse. She wants to meet him before giving him the job of designing her website. She reminds him a bit of Janine, or rather of how Janine might have grown to be in twenty years' time.

'I need to feel your vibrations,' she tells him when they meet in the Milkmaid coffee shop on the windswept front.

Some clients are like that. They want to establish a good personal relationship. Others just want it done as

72

cheaply and quickly as possible by email. Either way it doesn't bother Lee. He isn't fazed by Ella Jacobs' ethereal style or her fanciful talk of chakras and spiritual channels – as long as she pays the bill. But he pays the bill for their coffees and it is then that he discovers there is only one key clinking against the coins in his trouser pocket.

Ella Jacobs talks at him. 'I'm qualified in aromatherapy, massage, reiki, meditation – so I'll need a page for each skill.'

'Um.' *Maybe she won't look in the study. She knows she's not supposed to go in there.*

'I've brought some information sheets with me.' She thrusts papers at him. 'Will they be enough for you to work from?'

'Mmm.' *Could she be trusted not to look?*

'And I thought, colours, nice restful tones – pale lavender, soft green, rose ....I've put some suggestions on each sheet.'

He stares at the pages without seeing them. *Maybe she won't even notice the key in the lock.*

'What do you think?'

'What?' *But she's as sharp as a pin; she never misses a speck of dust or a smear on the windows.*

'Aren't you listening to me? I asked you what you thought.' *But if she does look, it will all be out in the open. I can't go on hiding them from each other forever.*

'Sorry, yes, you were saying?'

Ella Jacobs is staring at him, a wounded look in her eyes. 'Lee, I'm sorry but I don't feel we're making any connection with each other here.'

'Oh, no, I'm sure all this is fine.' He moves to pick up her papers but she grabs them back, holds them against her chest.

'I wouldn't be happy working with you; our rhythms don't seem to coincide at all.' She gets up to leave without finishing her coffee.

The finality of her movement reminds him of his last image of Janine as she marched away down The Haven's front path to her Mini, the back seat stuffed with her belongings.

'You dirty bastard,' Shazza shrieks as he comes through the open front door.

'You weren't supposed to go in there,' he mutters, trying to edge past her. His one fear is that she's done something to harm Petra, poor Petra who wouldn't hurt anyone.

'I knew you were up to something in there.' She pins him against the wall. Her voice is shaking as much as the finger she jabs in his chest.

'She isn't your rival,' he tries to console her.

'You've been sticking your cock in that – thing, all this time you've been doing me, haven't you?'

'No,' he lies. 'You don't understand. I was so lonely, after Janine left. I don't find it easy, meeting girls, chatting them up. When I met you, I already had Petra.'

'Petra?' she spits but her eyes soften. 'I should just fuck off and leave you right now, but…'

He sees her posture relax and takes the opportunity to start sidling down the hallway. She follows him into the study.

'Well it'll have to go,' she says.

She has thrown a sheet over Petra so Lee can't see the tennis whites he dressed her in this morning, the neat pleated skirt and frilly pants. Only her feet, in spotless white socks and plimsolls, stick out under the fabric, making her look like an athletic ghost.

'It's that thing or me.' Shazza draws herself up to her full five-foot-three and sticks her chin out. She cracks her chewing gum and gives Lee a hard stare.

Sadly he packs up Petra's clothes, her tongues, her makeup and stacks them in the boot of his car. Petra sits in the passenger seat, still covered by her sheet. It feels like history repeating itself.

'Take it to the tip and come straight back,' Shazza orders. 'I'll get some chips in for our lunch.'

At the end of the Plotlands road Lee turns left, away from the road that leads to the tip and instead heads for Flint and the M56. No way will Petra end up on a garbage heap. The least he can do is take her back to where she came from – to Love Unconditional, where they can find her a new home. Tears fill his eyes. He has to stop in a layby before they reach the motorway. When he feels calmer, he pulls off the sheet and rearranges Petra's clothes, her mussed up hair. Her eyes plead with him.

'I don't have any choice,' he whispers, brushing her cheek with his lips. If she stayed he would never have any peace, Shazza and Milly Pink would see to that. Giggles and whispers would follow him wherever he went.

Petra doesn't try to persuade him. He knows she accepts his decision. She always does. He takes her soft little hand in his. Life is about to change for them both. On the M56 he hesitates for a moment before taking the M6 turnoff instead of carrying on to Manchester. Petra seems to smile as he takes the exit for the M55 to Blackpool where sex toys and blow up dolls are ten a penny and where frankly, no one gives a damn.

Heart's Desire

Shazza was writing a shopping list. She had half an
hour to spare before catching the twelve o'clock bus to
Rhyl so she sat down in the garden with a cup of tea
and a fag and opened her notebook on a clean page.

1. *Must have his own place (nice and tidy).* She eyed
her auntie's crumbling prefab. That was definitely
number one, none of your crummy bedsits covered in
beer cans and smelly socks neither.

2. Must have a car. She was sick of waiting round
for those bloody buses that never came on time and
trundled round half the countryside before getting to
town. And in winter the service was so bad it was a
struggle to get there and back in a day. Should she put
down make and model? She wasn't really that bothered,
long as it got from A to B and didn't break down every
five minutes. She chewed the end of her pen for a
moment then wrote *fairly new, good condition.*

3. *Working or of independent means.* Independent
means sounded good. She'd got it from the Mills and
Boon she'd just finished reading where Lucy the stable
girl had caught the eye of Martin de Somerville, owner
of Hadley Hall, only it had turned out she wasn't really
a stablegirl, but an IT billionaire's daughter on a gap
year before studying at Cambridge. Shazza thought if
she had the chance of a gap year she'd opt for
something a bit more exotic like backpacking in
Australia or Bangkok, but then the whole story would
have to be changed wouldn't it? She looked at her

watch. Time was slipping by. She had to do her shopping and get home by lunchtime; she had the Williams sisters' house to clean at two o'clock.

4. *Must be good-looking.* Was it necessary? Shazza stubbed out her cigarette and sipped her tea. She knew she wasn't one of the world's great beauties so she wasn't going to be too fussy, but he'd have to be clean and someone you wouldn't be ashamed to be seen out with. Someone who'd appreciate a neat and tidy home, who wouldn't mind smoking in the garden instead of the house. But did he have to be her 'type' in fact did she really have a 'type'? She liked to read about men who were tall, dark and just a little bit rough with their women but she'd been attracted to all sorts of men, short and fair, even ginger as well as the dark, handsome ones who were always whisked off by someone sexier than herself. So maybe attraction didn't go in types and anyway, wasn't she looking for security rather than that all-encompassing love that everyone went on about?

She didn't want to think about that. How everyone went on about love, love, love as if it was everything. What did it mean? Was it love her mother had shown when she'd run off and left her with Aunty and Uncle? And what about them? They'd brought her up, done everything for her, she couldn't say they hadn't but had they really loved her? She'd never got the hugs and cuddles that she'd longed for.

There'd been her husband, Max but that had only lasted six months even though she'd loved him so much. Too much, he'd told her the day he went. 'I'm suffocating, drowning in it. You want to get a life.'

Well, she'd got one now, hadn't she, hiding out in this dump where there were no prospects apart from occasional single dads on holiday with their kids or retired pensioners with dreams of restored youth? Who wanted those? The ones she'd met that did live in Plotlands had been a sorry crew, all with something to hide. Look at that bloke Lee. He'd seemed so nice, so caring till she found out his dirty little secret, and the one before him, that Arnie had almost killed her. There'd been nothing about him to suggest he was a murderer. She thought about her own reasons for escaping to Plotlands but they hardly compared and anyway that was all in the past now. She'd made a fresh start but it seemed there'd been nothing but trouble since she came to Plotlands. After Arnie there'd been those awful murders in his bungalow with all those bikers and the bloke next door to him just vanished into thin air. She was beginning to feel isolated with the empty homes opposite hers and no sign of any new tenants.

She touched her face, feeling the dry skin on her cheeks, the creases round her eyes. It was too late to leave things to chance. Time to be organised, focus on what she should settle for. How would she feel if she married without love? It was too much to think about. She lit a fresh cig and turned her mind to her list. Was there anything else? She didn't want someone with boring hobbies like fishing or football or making boats out of matchsticks. She didn't really have any hobbies herself besides reading Mills and Boons, smoking and chewing gum, which hardly counted. It didn't do to be too precious either. She wanted someone with a bit of life left in him, to take her pubbing and clubbing but if she put that it sounded like she was a bit of a tramp. The philosophical problem of whether to marry for love or security was still niggling at the back of her mind. She would have to hurry or she'd miss the bus. She wrote

5. *Good personality* – and closed the notebook.

On the top deck of the bus she checked her real shopping list, making sure she'd put down a reminder to get her supply of Benson and Hedges from Mack the dodgy fag dealer in the indoor market. He might be a prospect for her list. He must have loads of money from all his dealings, he had his legit business with the market stall, must have transport and he was always going on foreign holidays to pick up cheap fags and booze. He wasn't much to look at and he never really looked clean but maybe he could be trained. Shazza made a mental note to find out if he was married or in a relationship.

In the market she stocked up on bleach and air fresheners. She treated herself to a new pair of long, dangly earrings, and put them on before approaching Mack's stall.

'Bloody cold now, isn't it?' He smiled as he handed over her regular cig order. How she loved that Welsh lilt. There was something about Welsh men, the way they looked at you properly, kind of warm.

'Soon be summer, bikini time,' she came back, flashing him a sexy smile and turning her head to show off her earrings.

'Bikini time any time for us, isn't it babe?' He winked at the blonde Shazza now saw standing behind her. 'Just got back from Tenerife. Give us a hand unpacking these boxes Di.'

Shazza took in the woman's tight jeans, the obviously enhanced boobs peeping from her low cut top, the bleached hair cascading over her shoulders. She ran her fingers through her own neat ponytail as Di went round to the back of the stall and hooked an arm possessively round Mack's waist.

'We're off to Portugal soon as it gets a bit warmer, aren't we hun?'

'Lucky you.' Shazza tucked her fags into her shopping trolley.

'Take care now cariad. See you next month.' Mack nodded at her and the light caught the gold ring in his left ear. Di's smile didn't waver but her eyes were hard. Shazza looked at their matching Mediterranean tans and sighed. She helped herself to one of their copy perfumes when Mack and Di turned their attentions to unpacking their boxes.

Up on the front a blustery wind whirled the sea into grey waves and played games with empty carrier bags and plastic chip trays along the pavements. Sharon stopped at Gypsy Rose's booth, a treat she allowed herself every so often when she had cash to spare. She liked the close intimacy of the little room, scarcely bigger than her broom cupboard at the bungalow, the exotic red velvet hangings. Gypsy Rose herself with her red headscarf and gold bangle earrings, her wise eyes peering through her dark eyeshadow, seemed imbued with strange power and mystery. Even though Shazza knew it was really a load of old rubbish, she kept returning. It was a place of possibilities.

Today Gypsy Rose was reading a newspaper and drinking a cup of coffee, both of which she hastily put aside when she saw she had a customer. 'What's it to be dear, cards, palm or crystal?' She gave no indication of recognising Shazza from her previous visits.

'Palm please.' Shazza parked her trolley with difficulty in the confined space and sat on the tiny stool opposite the fortune teller. She held out her hand after scrubbing it with a tissue from her pocket. Gypsy Rose peered at it for a long time. It was stuffy in the little box after being outside and Shazza wished she'd taken her coat off.

At last Gypsy Rose looked up. 'You've had a lucky escape dear, quite recently. Something bad happened, eh?'

What was she talking about? She wasn't supposed to say things like that. Shazza tried to pull her hand away but Gypsy Rose hung on like a bird of prey.

'Never mind dear, he wasn't the one for you.'

Shazza relaxed. Gypsy Rose was only on about Arnie. She'd thought she was getting somewhere with Arnie and he had seemed quite a nice man really. He wasn't much to look at but there had been something nice, something safe about him. She hadn't loved him; it was just that old security thing again. She'd told herself that love would come in time, and then just as she'd thought she'd got him on the hook, he'd shown his true colours, attacking her like that for no reason at all. Still, it had been a bigger shock when she'd learned he'd topped himself on the beach. She didn't believe for one moment that it had been an accident. Everyone who lived in Plotlands knew about the quicksands and how to avoid them. She'd told the chap from the local paper that when he'd come round – that must be how Gypsy Rose knew about it. She must have seen Shazza's photo in the paper. She'd almost believed the old fraud was psychic after all.

But that was quite a long time ago and Gypsy Rose hadn't mentioned it before so maybe she was on about Lee. She still didn't know where he'd got to after he disappeared that day with his bloody sex doll. A few weeks later a man in a white van had turned up and emptied the house, refusing to answer any questions about Lee's whereabouts. 'Well, good riddance,' she thought, peering at her hand as if she might see whatever Gypsy Rose could see.

'Never mind dear, it was all for the best in the end, eh?'

Shazza nodded, waiting for the usual promises – the tall, dark stranger, the unexpected inheritance. She wanted that reassurance.

'And now the way is clear for a new opportunity, something to bring your heart's desire. You deserve it. I can see you've worked hard in your life.'

Shazza nodded, tears threatening at the back of her eyes. It was true, all true. How she'd had to slave before she escaped to Aunty's bungalow. She'd thought it would be an easy touch, keeping house for old Mr Palmer but God, how wrong she'd been: that great house, filthy dirty and the grubby, incontinent old goat demanding her attention morning, noon and night. It had been his own fault, what had happened. He'd just been one in a long line of people working her like a dog. If he'd treated her a little better...

Gypsy Rose looked at her diamanté watch and let go of Shazza's hand. 'I can see a nice little bungalow by the sea.'

Shazza knew her time was up. The clairvoyant always finished with the same line, just as Shazza herself always made the same reply. 'I already got one, love.'

Outside, she stopped to light up a fag. Those tantalising words, 'a new opportunity' echoed in her mind. She hadn't noticed the little door in front of her before. It was freshly painted pink and grey, perhaps the reason it had caught her eye today. The sign on it read, 'Heart's Desire, Find Your Perfect Match.' Must be a new venture, she thought. Businesses started up and went bust in Rhyl all the time.

'A new opportunity.' She stared at the door. She'd tried a couple of online dating sites and she'd met a nice bloke on Facebook, leastways she'd thought he was nice till she gave him her mobile number and he sent her a photo of his penis.

But a proper dating agency – surely they'd have a better class of client, weed out all the losers and weirdos? It seemed like fate that she'd arrived here. It must be the new opportunity that Gypsy Rose saw; she'd even mentioned heart's desire. Shazza stubbed out her cig and went in.

At home she forced herself to put away her shopping before sitting down with the folder of printouts from Hearts' Desire. It was like magic. Two hours ago it had all been a dream and now here she was with three likely men lined up. They must be okay; the agency had selected them to match her personality and interests. And she had her pick; it was her choice, not theirs. That was important.

She ate her tuna sandwich with one eye on the clock. The Williams sisters were sticklers for timekeeping. There was just time to contact her first choice. She scanned the sheets but kept coming back to the photographs. Peter sounded like her type, had his own house and transport but Jonathon was better looking. Stuart, well Stuart looked a bit too posh for her but Sally, the girl at the agency had said he was perfect for her and he had a good job as a sales executive.

Should she phone or email first? It was such a big step. Email seemed easier to break the ice but she needed personal contact to make it real for her, but which one? It was getting late, she really needed to go.

She picked up her pen, closed her eyes and dropped it down on the papers. It landed on Jonathon.

She should have known by his eagerness when she phoned him that the date would not go well. From long experience she could spot a mummy's boy a mile off. With his neatly pressed old-fashioned suit and slicked down hair, she could almost see the impression of his mother's lipstick on his forehead, where she'd kissed him goodbye before sending him off. Jonathon liked to be called Jonathon, not Jon. He worked in a flour mill which probably explained why he could only afford to take her to a seafront fish and chip restaurant. She watched him counting out the money for their meal from a small leather purse and sighed.

It was a pity because he had the face of a cherub with wonderful sapphire eyes you could drown in. She thought of Martin de Somerville and had to drag herself back to the reality of the drone in her ear about Jonathon's mother's activities in their local church and his sister's job in Prestatyn library. On his fifth visit to the loo, which he called the lavatory, she made a discreet escape.

Back at home, she tore up Jonathon's printout. She should have stuck with her first instincts and gone with Peter. This time she decided to be more cautious and email first. She attached a photo of herself, a nice one her friend Martine had taken on the beach at Salou. That seemed so long ago now, must be seven years at least. How time flies, she thought, wondering what Martine was doing now. She'd left them all behind, her old friends, what family she had. She'd had to leave quickly with the old goat catching her red-handed and she was too scared to contact anyone, too afraid it would all catch up with her. Here she had no one really, not since Lee had gone, despite going to the bingo and the karaoke on Saturday nights. They were friendly enough, the locals, but maybe she just hadn't been there long enough to fit in. Maybe in twenty years' time – she shuddered at the thought of long empty years with that bleak seascape in front of her as she aged and stiffened in Aunty's rotting bungalow, surrounded by empty, decaying properties.

The reply came back within an hour. Another eager beaver, she thought but her heart still thudded in anticipation as she clicked the message open.

Hey Babe, you look like a dreem. I've been wating for a gril like you. Let's meat up if we get on we culd go for a run. How about the Sarasen on Wensdy 8.00. Its rock nite, hope you lik rock.

Complimentary but not sleazy. Maybe the spelling mistakes were just the way people wrote emails now, like texts. She liked that little bit of doubt – 'if we get on', not taking her for granted. 'Go for a run'? For a moment the phrase struck her with horror, what if he turned up in shorts and bandanna, expecting her to jog for miles along the prom? No – she laughed at herself. He meant in his car, of course he did. The Sarasen? She had to think for a minute then she remembered the old Palace pub out on the east end of the front. It had been taken over, done up and renamed the Saracen. Now it was a popular meeting place for the younger pubbers, selling brightly coloured drinks and hosting different music nights, quizzes and fancy dress parties. She wasn't really one for rock, preferred more romantic stuff but she didn't mind a bit of Elvis or even Status Quo.

She pored over Peter's photo; really he was quite attractive with his fashionable stubble and blond gelled up hair – looked a bit like Sting only chubbier round the chin. She spent hours scrutinising the message and photo, more hours composing her own reply before she finally clicked the Send button, confirming that she'd be there. The night was almost over by the time she went to bed, a thin line of light breaking on the horizon.

One look told her she wouldn't be going for a run in a luxury car, nor would she be jogging on the prom. And this was before she even got inside the Saracen. Frenzied music blared from the entrance and most of the clientele were out on the pavement: smoking, swigging pints, spitting and swearing. Shazza took in the leathers, the big boots and realised she'd made a big mistake. But even as she turned to go, a great paw landed on her arm and a voice boomed, 'Sharon' in a cloud of garlicky breath behind her.

Peter's chin was not the only chubby thing about him. No wonder he'd only sent a head and shoulders photo. Shazza looked up at this giant of a man. She forced a smile as she realised he must weigh at least twenty-five stone. The thought of groping all that flesh, let alone having it on top of her, made her quiver. She couldn't escape, his bulk blocked her path.

'You look gorgeous,' he growled, 'good enough to eat.' His mouth opened in a wide grin as if he really was thinking about gobbling her up.

Shazza's belly lurched as she imagined his large and very white teeth biting into her tender parts.

'C'mon babe, let's go inside, where it's more – intimate.' He winked at her suggestively then steered her over the threshold, holding on to her as if she were a prize and pushed her into a seat in the half-empty bar.

'What's it to be girl, anything you like?'

'Just a Coke please,' Shazza had the feeling she was going to need her wits about her.

While Peter was at the bar, his ham-like arms waving as he chatted to the barmaid, she looked round the room. A group of girls in jeans were doing the wanking horse to the earsplitting music, their long hair flopping like mops. Big men with beards guffawed at nearby tables. They eyed Shazza, grinned and laughed some more but fell respectfully silent when Peter returned with the drinks.

Conversation was impossible with the noise going on but after a few exchanges she learned that Peter had three kids in Cwmbran that he hardly ever saw.

'How come?' she asked but his reply was lost in a crescendo of shrieks as the music reached a climax.

'Never mind me, let's talk about you,' came through quite clearly. She couldn't talk about her real past and thankfully whatever she said he wouldn't be able to hear her so she began to tell him how she was looking for a charming prince and a fairytale romance. When the music suddenly stopped, her words, '– someone to love me,' floated out across the silence. The dancers, pushing their hair back into order, stared at her. The men stroked their beards and they stared too.

'C'mon,' Peter said, 'let's get outta here.' His eyes were kind and she realised with gratitude that he hadn't tried to grope her, hadn't even touched her. But what would happen outside? 'I want to show you my other girl.' He turned back and for a moment she thought she saw the real man under the macho stance, then he gave a great belly laugh. 'You'll have to get used to her.'

The bike gleamed with polished care. Shazza stared at the death's head, circled with flames that graced the tank.

'Harley low rider,' Peter said, running lover's hands over the handlebars. 'Not dressed for a run, are you?' He handed her a helmet, looked doubtfully at her tight skirt and three inch heels. 'Ever been on a bike before?'

She shook her head.

'Better wear my jacket. I'm used to the cold.' He folded her tenderly into the oversized leather and she was grateful for it in the cool night, even though it carried his animal warmth and smelled of sweat mixed with deodorant. He pushed her fumbling fingers away from the helmet straps and fixed it with a few deft movements before fitting his clumsy leather gauntlets on her hands.

'Hop on then,' he shouted, once he was astride the growling bike. Shazza hitched up her skirt and prayed. 'Just hold on to me and lean when I lean,' he called and the bike shot off with a jerk, almost throwing her off there and then.

Why was she doing this? It was the opposite of everything she wanted but there was something new and exciting about it. After a few attempts she succeeded in sitting on the tiny back seat and getting her heels to lodge behind the foot pedals. She'd never thought she could be so cold as freezing air rushed round her, up her hiked skirt and into places it should never be. She slithered about on the high seat, which seemed intent on biting between her legs, reluctant to make contact with Peter's broad back but she was so afraid of falling off that eventually she gave in and clung to him, her arms barely reaching round his sides.

Thankfully, the trip was short; the couple of times they banked for a bend she was sure they would both fall off. 'You leaned the wrong way,' he laughed, as they pulled up at a secluded spot near Ffrith Beach.

'I was terrified,' she was laughing too but with hysteria as she struggled to get off the bike and pull off the constricting helmet.

'You'll learn,' he ruffled her hair, traced her cheek with his finger. 'You've got some colour now.' He lit two cigs and gave her one of them.

They both leaned on the handrail, looking out at the dark sea, where the occasional white wavecrest could still be seen. Shazza kept recalling his touch on her cheek; it had been so gentle, not what she had expected at all.

'What I told you before – about Heather, my ex – I made a mistake.'

He must be talking about the conversation in the pub, when she couldn't hear a thing but just kept nodding.

'We all make mistakes,' she said to cover up her ignorance.

'It was my fault. I shouldn't have hit her. It was only a tap, but I shouldn't have done it. I'd give anything to be able to take it back.'

Shazza dragged on her cig. She wanted a stick of gum but it didn't seem right, chewing on a first date. What was she supposed to say?

'It taught me something.' He wasn't looking at her; his face was turned to the sea. 'Some mistakes can't be put right. You just have to learn from them and move on.' He flicked his cigarette into the water. 'Just wanted you to know that, right from the start.'

There was only the sound of little waves slapping against the breakwater. Shazza couldn't think of a reply. She tossed her cig after his, then he turned to her and crushed her in his arms. Despite that, his mouth was tender on hers, his tongue gently exploring. She began to respond until his hand crept under her top, massaging her breast, while the other squeezed her buttocks before reaching down to the hem of her skirt.

She remembered Aunty's advice about violent men. 'Leopards don't change their spots' and a sudden memory came of the panicked moment when she'd clawed Arnie's fingers from her throat. She pushed Peter away, hoping against hope that the tenderness he'd shown her was real, because here in the middle of nowhere, she'd have no chance against his strength.

'I like you, Sharon,' he said leaning on the handrail and zipping her back into his jacket. 'I don't like a girl that gives it away on a first date.'

Looks don't mean a thing, Shazza thought on the ride back to Plotlands. The night hadn't been a total disaster but she didn't quite know what to make of Peter. She leaned against his back and thought she might consult Gypsy Rose about him but she didn't let him see where she lived, making him drop her off outside Milly Pink's house. She crept round the back and hid behind Milly's shed till the roar of the Harley faded into the distance.

In her own living room, she settled down with a cup of tea and chewed long and hard on a stick of gum before she filed Peter away with a maybe. There was still Stuart and he might turn out to be the man of her dreams.

She ordered a new dress from her mail order catalogue for their first date at Mariners' Wharf, a posh restaurant at the better end of the seafront. She had to buy new shoes too as she'd broken the heel off her good ones getting off Peter's motorbike. She was too excited to worry about how many sessions she'd have to do for the Williams sisters and Milly Pink in order to pay for it all. If only she could get a proper job, like cleaning in the comprehensive school at Prestatyn, her life would be so much more secure, but if she went legit she'd be traceable and she was sure they'd still be looking for her – old Mr. Palmer wasn't one to let things drop.

Her mind wandered to finding the right shade of lipstick to go with her new shoes and whether to wear a jacket or the fringed stole Aunty had given her two Christmases ago before she'd started to go funny. She decided on the stole, after all Spring was coming in and Stuart was going to collect her in his car. She dabbed herself with Mack's perfume and made herself look intriguing with the jade green eyeshadow she'd lifted from Boots on an earlier shopping trip.

Stuart's neat suit and the nearly new Toyota Ayris told her that she'd made the right decision abandoning the other two. Her latest Mills & Boon featured an auburn hero, a gambler in stocks and shares, so she didn't mind that Stuart lacked the saturnine dark looks she idealised and the way his hair flopped over his left eye was pretty cute. Selling paint wasn't very glamorous but it was a steady job. She appreciated that and at least he didn't go on and on about it.

'So what about you, what do you do?' he asked over the seafood starter.

'Run my own cleaning business,' She looked him candidly in the eye.

'Self-employed? That's brave in these uncertain times.' He placed a prawn neatly in his mouth. 'But then I suppose it's a good market, people always need cleaners. How many do you have working for you?'

'Only me at the moment, but I'm planning to expand.'

'Sensible.' He smiled. 'Best to build up gradually; don't take on too much debt.'

She nodded, almost choking when he added,

'So, have you always lived round here? You don't have the local accent.'

'No, I'm from Liverpool, staying at my aunt's old place.'

'What made you move here? I'd have thought you'd do better in Liverpool, businesswise I mean.'

Shazza thought quickly. 'Accommodation's expensive. I can stay at my aunt's place for free, kind of like a caretaker. She's in a home now, she can't keep the bungalow up to scratch. And anyway there's plenty of work here, looking after the caravans on the camps.'

'It's a nice place, Plotlands, but it's a bit of a backwater. A lot of the old residents moved out. Last time I went there were quite a few empty places.' He finished his starter and pushed his plate away.

'Oh, I love it,' Sharon lied. 'We used to come here for holidays when I was a kid.'

'Nostalgia eh? What about your parents, brothers and sisters?'

God this bloke was nosy. 'No,' she said, letting a note of exasperation into her voice. 'My parents are dead.'

'You're not married then, no children?'

'No. I was married but it didn't work out. I'm divorced now.'

'Me too, I expect the agency told you that. I don't see her any more. Don't see much of my family either; my sister lives in Australia now. I suppose I'm a bit lonely, hence Heart's Desire.'

Shazza nodded, thankful to get him talking about himself. The less said about her own past, the better.

'I know,' she said and it seemed as if they shared the same longing for romance, even love. Over their surf'n'turf he changed the subject to their likes and dislikes and Shazza felt more comfortable. She began to have a good time. When he dropped her off at home without even attempting to invite himself in, she thought that maybe this time things might work out. Heart's Desire had been right. He was perfect for her.

That night she dreamed of the day her mother had come back for her. Shazza had been nine and she'd been naughty that morning, confined to her bedroom in disgrace. When her mother came to the door, Shazza peered out of the window but didn't know who she was. She understood enough of the shouting and screaming that followed to piece things together. The next thing she knew, the woman came running up the stairs and grabbed her, hugging and kissing her, covering her with the smell of her perfume and lipstick. Before she could make sense of what was going on, she found herself being dragged down the front path away from her aunty and into a car with a strange man at the wheel. She'd sat in the back of the car while the man drove off and he and her mother argued.

'You didn't say nothing about taking on no kid,' he kept shouting and her mother cried and kept saying, 'Oh Ray, what else could I do, she's my flesh and blood?'

'Well, I ain't up for it,' the man said, and seeing her mother crying, Shazza burst into tears herself. This made the man even angrier. 'See what I mean,' he said and wrenched at the steering wheel so the car fishtailed about and made Shazza feel sick.

'Never mind, sweetie, I'll always be with you now,' Shazza's mother said. She kept leaning back over the seat and stroking Shazza's hair as if she were a puppy but what she said wasn't true. After they had driven round for a long time with Ray and her mother shouting at each other the whole time, they'd stopped at a railway station and Shazza's mother had taken her into the ladies' waiting room.

'I'll just go and get you some chocolate,' she said, 'stay there like a good girl. I'll be back in a minute.'

Flesh and blood or no flesh and blood that was the last Shazza ever saw of her. She'd been hysterical by the time the station staff found her and returned her to her aunt like a lost dog. That minute had stretched out over the years and although she knew her mother wasn't ever coming back, her dream self kept resurrecting her ever so often. Was that what love was about? Shazza thought, waking up to a pillow wet with tears.

After two more dates, Shazza was sure she was on the right track. Stuart brought flowers and chocolates. On their third date, she brought him in for coffee, kisses and cuddles. She could have gone further, she wanted to, she so loved to be held, but she remembered Max and even Arnie with their demands for time to be alone. No, she would play this one carefully, this time everything was going so well.

Until one day she returned from town and dropped into Milly Pink's shop because she'd forgotten her supply of chewing gum.

'Someone's been asking for you,' Milly said as she counted out Shazza's change. 'Posh feller in a suit.'

'Did he have reddish, floppy hair?' Shazza's thoughts were on Stuart. She was still pondering Gypsy Rose's latest prediction that a surprise was due in the immediate future and she wondered if it might be in the form of a marriage proposal.

'Nah, dark, smart alecky type. Looked like some kind of official.'

Shazza's mouth fell open, showing her wad of gum. She closed it again quickly, licking her lips. 'What did he say?'

'Nothing much.' Milly handed the money over. 'Just asked if I knew when you'd be in. I didn't say nothing.' She looked up slyly.

She can't know, Shazza thought but then her face was giving her away and her breathing had turned fast and shallow.

'Thanks.' She pocketed her change and left. At home she was too upset to unpack her shopping. She lit a cig and paced up and down peering out of the windows in case the dreaded stranger was lurking behind a bush. Her past had caught up with her at last, it could mean nothing else – or could it? Maybe it was just someone from the electricity board or from BT, come to check Aunty's phone. She'd just about calmed herself down, made herself put the kettle on for coffee when a loud knock, a rentman's knock as her aunty used to say, almost stopped her heart.

Instinctively she hid under the kitchen table, even though the kitchen was at the back of the house. If she stayed quiet as a mouse, whoever it was might go away. Another loud knock, then silence. Shazza began to think about crawling out of her hidey hole; the kettle was cooling, having switched itself off and her knees were killing her. She poked her head out and saw a man in a suit, staring through the kitchen window at her.

Only when he moved towards the back door did she remember that she'd forgotten to lock it when she'd come in.

'Sharon Blake?'

'She's not here, I'm the cleaner.'

'Oh come on, love, I've got your photo.'

Shazza chewed her gum, weighing up how to react. Was it best to come out all guns firing, or dissolve into tears?

He seemed encouraged by her silence, pulling out one of her (or rather Aunty's) kitchen chairs and sitting himself down as if he owned the place. 'What about a cup of tea, then we can have a chat?'

Shazza obeyed, her mind working furiously all the time. It was a shock, even though she'd half expected it, ever since she escaped to Plotlands but as time had gone by she'd begun to think she was going to get away with it – now this, just when life seemed to be taking a turn for the better. Tears trickled out of her eyes.

'Turn the taps off, love, Mr Palmer just wants his money back.'

'It was only a bit here and there,' she plonked the mug of tea in front of him. She couldn't face a cup herself, instead she lit a fresh cig and glared at him.

'Don't you want to know who I am?' he grinned, full of confidence now he'd got her where he wanted her. He had those saturnine looks she liked so much, black hair with green eyes, but dark and nasty. 'Paul Standish, private investigator.' He flipped a card across the table. 'A bit here and there – but it added up, Sharon. It was too easy, wasn't it?'

'He was so stingy.' Sharon stopped crying as she thought about the injustices of working for Mr Palmer. 'I bet he didn't tell you what he expected me to do for his measly pay: cooking, cleaning, washing, mopping up his incontinent mess.'

'Oh, I can sympathise.' The green eyes looked lazily at her. 'But the fact is, I work for Mr Palmer and there it is, I'm here to get the money back.'

'How did you find me?' Shazza lit another cig with difficulty. Her hands were shaking.

'Took me a while, you covered your tracks pretty good. I got my methods though. Wouldn't do to tell my secrets, would it?'

'I can't pay it back.' She pleaded with her eyes. 'You can see I got nothing. This place is my aunty's.'

'I know,' he said sadly, 'but the choice is yours. You pay it back or Mr P gets the police in.'

Shazza dissolved into tears. 'I told you, I haven't got it.'

'Look,' he reached out and patted her hand. 'I'm not a monster, it's just my job. Tell you what, I'll give you twenty-four hours, see what you can rustle up, eh?'

What could she do but agree? After he'd left she sat chewing gum and smoking cig after cig. Everything had been going so well, now it was all gone in a puff of smoke. The identity she'd carefully begun to build – lost. Who would want to know her once she was branded as a thief? Certainly not Stuart.

There was no one she could turn to for help, Aunty was too far gone and she hadn't any money anyway and what she did have was locked away in the care home. No, Paul Standish had given her one chance and she had to take it. Did he really think she was going to stick around till he came back? He seemed too streetwise for that; somehow she got the feeling he was giving her the opportunity to escape. Maybe he really did feel sorry for her.

She spent the evening packing her things into the trolley suitcase she'd arrived with eighteen months earlier; except for the new dress and shoes, there wasn't much more nor less than she had come with. It was no use asking herself where she would go, lucky that the Williams sisters had paid her the day before. She looked at her shopping, still in the trolley. She could have saved herself the money, if only she'd known. Gypsy Rose for once had been spot on with her prediction.

In bed, she tossed and turned thinking of Stuart and how he would never know why she'd deserted him. The nice home she'd imagined them sharing disappeared into the mist of her unknown future and tomorrow was just an empty space beyond the bus stop. There would be a choice of sorts: one way the bus went to Rhyl, the other way to Flint.

In the dream, she waited at the bus stop, straining her eyes for the blue flash of the bus as it turned the bend at the railway bridge and began the long straight approach down the Plotlands road but instead a flare of red caught her eye. A bright red sports car flew towards her. A woman was driving, her long hair blowing.

Shazza's mouth dried, formed the word, Mother, but nothing came out. Her mother was smiling.

'Told you I'd come back for you,' she braked and pulled up sharply.

Shazza felt so light she could have floated up to the sky. She started to lift her trolley.

'Oh, won't be a minute,' her mother said, revving the engine, 'just getting some chocolate.' She drove away, the roar of the engine drowning Shazza's wail of despair. Shazza peered after the car as it turned the corner by Milly Pink's shop and she stood on tiptoe, waiting for its return. It had to come back. There was only one way out of Plotlands.

She breathed a sigh of relief as it came into sight again. This time it would be all right. But when she looked closer, Paul Standish was at the wheel. Terror seized her but the bus was now trundling towards her. 'Hurry up,' she prayed, hopping with anxiety. The bus doors wheezed open just as the red sports car screeched to a halt.

At seven-twenty the next morning she waited at the bus stop, eyes peeled for a flash of red. The dream had been so real, it had seemed like a prophecy but all she saw was the streak of blue as the bus made its leisurely way to the stop. The direction board showed it was bound for Rhyl.

Shazza took a last look up and down the road.

'You getting on or what?' the driver huffed. He watched her struggle to lift the heavy trolley, sighed as she rummaged in her purse for change.

The bus was empty except for one old man who appeared to be asleep. Shazza parked her trolley in the luggage bay. She sat down and broke out a fresh stick of gum as the familiar landscape slid past.

Beloved Sally

Why had they come here? Sally had said that the peace and quiet would do him good. She'd said that he would feel safe but she was wrong.

Julian stared out across the bare Plotlands beach at the place where a dim line denoted the distant flop of wavelets breaking on the sands, a vague colour change from beigey brown to beigey grey. A single swan flew out towards the sea. To his right, the Questrol gas terminal jutted into the sky, like an invading monster from some dystopian future. Julian stretched his hands inside his army greatcoat pockets. The cold bit through into his fingers. He'd forgotten his gloves.

The trouble with Plotlands was that the land came to a stop and there was no escape, nowhere to run. He could feel them at his back, all those staring eyes, just waiting to catch him off guard. He wouldn't let it happen. He had to be vigilant every moment but it was so hard. He was so tired of trying to keep his eyes open every night. He daren't sleep because they were always waiting for him to make a mistake, to slip, even for a second.

Only when Sally promised to stay on guard could he close his eyes for a few moments but now he couldn't even be sure of her. Two nights earlier he'd woken at 2 a.m. and found her asleep, leaving him vulnerable. 'Just nodded off,' she'd said. Since then he hadn't slept at all. He just couldn't trust her. What if that solicitude, that care for him, persuading him to come here, had all been a plot, part of a plan to get him where he'd be helpless… or so they thought?

No, he couldn't let up. There must be others beside himself and it was up to him to find them, save them if he had to. How was he to do it? He was one solitary man in all this bleakness. He lifted his arms to the white sky but it was empty. No help was coming. He couldn't pray to God. God had abandoned the world.

He turned and saw Sally standing a little way off, watching. How long had she been there? She started towards him, a smile on her face.

'Come on Jools.' She came up, linked her arm through his. 'It's bloody freezing. Let's go home and get you a hot drink.'

In the house, he watched her move around the kitchen. Lovely– it was the only word for her, the graceful way she carried herself. Everyone had been surprised when she married him, none more so than he– and the way she'd stuck with him. It was almost too good to be true. She was too good to be true. For a moment he saw something alien in her eyes and his heart hammered. She was his only armour against the rest of them. If she was false, what chance did he have?

She put a steaming mug of coffee in front of him. He looked at her as she sat down opposite him and she was just his wife, Sally. But he remembered she hadn't batted an eyelid when that woman Sharon had disappeared, and she hadn't been the first. There was that greasy bloke with the dead motorbike, there one day, gone the next and no one knew anything about it and he'd overheard them gossiping in Milly Pink's shop about another one swallowed up in the quicksand. That must have been before he and Sally had come there. There'd been those murders too, but they'd never found the bodies. It was strange that they'd left the feet, it wasn't like them to be so careless. The police had pinned the murders on some biker bloke but Julian knew better, although of course, he too might have been one of them.

Those disappearances puzzled him at first because once they'd been taken over, converted, he knew for a fact that they came back and carried on as normal. All the time their numbers were growing. They were biding their time, gathering strength. After a while he got it figured out. The ones who disappeared must have been resistant, like him; must have sussed out their game and they'd had to be disposed of, just as they'd like to dispose of him. Those others hadn't been clever enough. He wasn't going to make that mistake. It wasn't for his own sake, his own survival; the fate of the world rested on his shoulders. He thought of the world taken over, its people enslaved and tears tricked him into showing his emotion. Humans were doomed unless he stood firm; they were too kind, too trusting. Like Sally – he looked at her uncertainly.

Sally was smiling her wonderful smile. She opened her mouth and showed him her teeth. 'Shall we go out somewhere tomorrow? Somewhere quiet, just for a change of scene? I was thinking about Bala.'

Was it a trap? To get him somewhere where he might relax. That weekend away Sally had, supposedly visiting her sister in Liverpool – had they taken her then or had she been one of them before he'd met her? Perhaps their meeting even had been contrived, if they'd known how special he was, how he was chosen to be their arch enemy. If it was true, they'd done a good job, he couldn't tell and he was expert at picking them out. And he didn't want to believe it, he'd come to love her so much. 'What are you thinking?' he said to himself. 'She's your wife.' But even as he thought this, he was looking at her perfect features, wondering if he reached out and pulled her skin would it peel back to reveal the bulging eyed alien beneath like in one of those old sci-fi films.

'If you like,' he said, reaching across the table to stroke her face. For now he had to trust her but he would have to watch her.

On the way back from Bala he dozed in the car; after all, how could they get him in there? He woke feeling refreshed as they passed through Denbigh and sat quietly watching Sally drive, admiring her regular profile.

She turned her head, swinging her hair, smiled at him. 'You've slept all the way back – you look so relaxed.'

It was true, he felt relaxed, safe in the warm car, Sally at his side. Outside, trees waved in an angry wind as they passed and rain began to batter the windows. If only they could stay like this, Julian thought as his eyes closed again.

At home there was no milk left for coffee. Sally wanted a bath so Julian had to go to Milly Pink's shop, much as he hated the place. They were all in there as usual, pretending to gossip but secretly exchanging real information, reporting back to Milly Pink who presided over them like a great fat spider. He was sure she was the ringleader, the head of their group or cell or whatever they called themselves. He'd stake his life she had some sort of communication device in the back room, some way of sending reports back to their masters. It wouldn't be a computer or anything traceable like that, more like something that could utilise waves between their planet and Earth, waves that human technology hadn't discovered. That was why he always felt funny in the shop; the concentration of the alien waves must be affecting the atmosphere inside.

As he walked in, silence fell and they all stared but he was used to that. Milly Pink put on a plastic smile as he helped himself to a carton of milk from the cooler. He counted out the money without a word.

'Sally all right, is she?' Milly Pink said, ringing up his purchase on her till.

'Fine,' he muttered. He didn't dare look in her cold, lizard eyes. If he did, she would know that he knew and it was important for them to think they were undetected, give them a false sense of security.

The buzz of their voices resumed as he left the shop, clanging the door behind him. He looked down at the money in his hand, realised she'd given him the wrong change. His immediate reaction was to ignore it. He knew she'd done it deliberately, perhaps the alien waves in the shop could somehow read his mind or affect him in some way and it was her way of keeping him in there. On the other hand it could be a test to find out if he knew about her real nature. If he didn't go back and complain she would know he was aware of the waves, of her plotting with her masters. Reluctantly he turned back into the shop. Silence descended again and this time the stares were openly hostile.

'You gave me the wrong change.' He held out his hand.

Milly looked at him suspiciously. 'I don't think so. I never make mistakes.'

'Well you have this time. Look.' He counted out the change.

'I'm sure I gave you the right money,' she huffed but she looked flustered. She opened the till, looked at the money inside. She didn't seem to know what to do next.

'Pretending tactics,' thought Julian. 'She's trying to keep me in here.' He felt distinctly peculiar; his head seemed to be whooshing as if something was passing through it, interfering with his thoughts. He thought about running out but he couldn't do that with them all standing staring and perhaps he was wrong altogether. They didn't want to keep him in there but to keep him away, make him feel so sick that he wouldn't go in there any more, so that he would leave them in peace to get on with their plotting and planning.

'You'll have to wait while I check the till.' Red spots had appeared on Milly's cheeks. She began laboriously to count the money in the different sections of the till.

Nobody spoke while this went on for the longest time. Julian wished he hadn't come back in the shop.

'Well,' Milly said at last, closing the till drawer. 'I wouldn't have believed it but you're right.' She held out some coins to him, pushing them into his hand as if begrudged. The scaly, alien look had gone off her face and she looked like a confused old lady, cheeks pink with embarrassment. 'I'm sorry,' she said with visible effort.

Julian shoved the money in his pocket and fled. He didn't slow down until he'd turned out of   Second Avenue onto the main Plotlands road which stretched straight ahead, empty except for a single black dot, someone walking in the distance. He passed the amusement arcade and the gift shop, both shuttered now for the winter, and crossed over by the public conveniences which remained open for people who came to walk their dogs or watch birds along the beach path. The black dot grew bigger, morphed into a walking figure, but not big enough to be an adult. Julian watched the small boy approach.

Small children were rarely seen in Plotlands once the tourist season was over. He guessed the boy was about eight or nine at the most. As they drew level with each other, the child dropped the money he'd been holding and the coins scattered round Julian's feet.

'Oh, shit,' said the boy, kneeling down and beginning to gather them up. Julian bent down to help. 'Thanks mate,' the child said, straightening up. 'Me nan'd kill me if I lost any.' He counted the coins in his hand then turned grateful eyes up to Julian whose heart lifted as he saw the boy was as normal as he was.

'Where do you live?' he asked.

'Chester,' the boy answered. I'm staying with me nan. Me mum's in the hospital. She's had a noperation. It's only for a few days, I hope.'

Alarm flooded Julian's brain. The kid was obviously in danger. 'What's your nan's name?' he asked, trying to keep the fear out of his voice.

'Mrs. Glover – Doris. She lives over there...' he pointed in the direction of Fourth Avenue. 'She's all right really.'

No she's not, Julian thought. Either the mother was one of them, or the grandmother had fooled her into letting her take the boy. He was here for conversion then he'd be returned, seeded into his home community to lay plans for invasion there. Julian thought what it would mean if he acted and blew his cover but this was important. If he did nothing, not only would the boy be lost but he'd be returned into normal society, a catalyst that would set off a whole new network of infection.

'Are you going to the shop?'

The boy nodded.

'What for?'

'Me nan sent me for her Woman's Weekly – and a Fray Bentos pie for our supper.' He said this carefully as if he had been made to memorise it. Could it be a secret message to Milly Pink?

'You mustn't go in there.' He went to grab the boy's arm but the boy dodged back.

'Why not?' His open expression changed to one of suspicion.

'They'll get you if you do.' Julian could see the kid didn't believe him.

'Me nan'll get me if I don't,' he went to push past Julian.

'You wouldn't want them to hurt you. They've got rays.' Julian succeeded in catching the boy's arm but the boy was too surprised to protest.

'Rays?' Julian knew he was thinking over films he had seen or computer games he played.

'Where's their spaceship then?' the boy said, giving Julian an I've-got-you- now look.

Julian had a sudden brainwave. 'It's on the beach,' he said, 'come on, I'll show you.'

'But I've got to go the message for me nan,' the boy said, although his eyes gleamed with excitement. 'And I'm not supposed to go anywhere with strange men.'

'I'm not strange am I? I only live over there.' He waved towards Third Avenue. 'Your nan knows me. And after I've shown you the spaceship you can go to the shop. It won't take a minute and I'll treat you to some sweets. What're your favourites?'

'Coca cola bottles,' the boy said, brightening, 'oh and those fried egg ones.'

'My name's Julian, what's yours?'

'Harry,' the kid said, squinting up at him.

'Okay Harry, come on then.' Julian walked off towards the beach.

108

'All right,' Harry said and trotted after him.

'It's a long way,' Harry said, dragging his feet and looking back along the empty path that ran above the beach.

'Nearly there,' Julian said. He wanted to take the boy by the hand to make sure he didn't run off but he didn't want to frighten him. The kid might think he was a paedophile. He pointed to the dilapidated wooden shed hiding amongst loops of brambles. It had once belonged to the regional water company but it had long since been abandoned. Julian sometimes sat in it when he wanted to hide and no one ever came there. He'd left the door ajar on his last visit and it still hung open, the heavy bar used to secure it from the outside, still propped up against the wall.

'That's not a spaceship,' Harry said scornfully.

'It's disguised,' Julian said. 'You don't think they'd let everyone see it, do you?'

Harry pondered this, then light broke across his face. 'You mean like the Tardis?'

'Exactly,' Julian said.

Harry jigged with excitement. 'Are you Dr. Who?'

'No,' Julian said, 'but I do the same kind of job.'

'Bloody hell,' Harry said admiringly. He rushed down the slope towards the shed and went in.

'Hey, there's nothing here,' he turned back.

Julian slammed the door shut and dropped the heavy bar into its slots. The windows were boarded up so there was no way the boy could get out and even though he was already hollering, no one would hear him there.

'It's for your own good,' Julian shouted over the boy's screams. 'Don't worry, I won't be long.' He ran all the way back to Milly Pink's shop, arriving out of breath. He bought more milk, cans of Coke, chocolate bars and crisps, then stopping at the sweet display, added a mixed bag of cola bottles and fried eggs.

Milly Pink paid him little attention. She resumed her conversation with a grizzled old woman he vaguely recognised as living in the bungalow next to the community centre. It was all about the amount of dogturds left by thoughtless owners of dogs in and around the nature reserve.

'Terrible, terrible,' the old woman kept saying.

'They should be ashamed of themselves,' Milly Pink said. 'Four pounds fifty-seven please.' She took Julian's five pound note and gave him a look that dared him to mention the mistake she'd made earlier with his change.

'They should be bloody prosecuted,' the old woman said, looking Julian up and down as if he might have a guilty dog hidden in his jacket.

The door clanged and a fat woman with purple hair rushed in. 'Has our Harry been in?' she gasped.

Milly Pink shook her head.

'I'll kill him when I get my hands on him,' the woman exclaimed. 'I told him, straight there and straight back.'

Julian slipped out and left them to it.

He only opened the shed door a fraction, just enough to push the bag of goodies in, because as soon as the lad heard Julian outside, he began beating on the door and screaming, 'Let me out, me nan'll kill me.'

'I can't,' Julian said into the gap. 'I'm not going to hurt you.'

'You are,' Harry shouted. 'There isn't no spaceship. You're after my body.' His voice rose high with terror, causing a similar fear to course through Julian. The door shuddered but held as the boy rained kicks from the inside.

'Stop it, stop it,' Julian hissed. 'I told you I won't hurt you. I'm trying to help you.'

The kicking stopped and the boy's screams dropped to sobs and then his voice came in a whine. 'Let me out, Julian, I won't tell no one, honest.'

'I can't.' Julian said. 'Look, I have to go but I'll be back for you later.' Quickly he shut the door and bolted it again. He ran, away from the boy's terror, away from his own horror at what he was doing, until he came to one of the picnic benches set along the top path, facing out to the sea. He slumped down, wiped a hand over his sweating face, only to find it was wet with tears. Gulping, he looked out at the quiet beach as the heat of his body subsided in the cold air. Far in the distance the sea glittered, a line at the end of the world.

When he got home with the milk it was almost dark. Sally was cross. 'You've been ages. You knew I was waiting for the milk.'

'I went for a bit of a walk, get some fresh air,' he muttered. 'I wasn't feeling too good, got a bit car sick on the drive home this afternoon.'

Her face softened. 'You look tired, why don't you have another nap while I get supper ready?'

Was this a trap to get him in his sleep? Did they already know he was moving against them? But he

111

went into the bedroom and lay down, glad of the space to think while he tried to figure out what to do next. All his nerves were jangling yet there was a kind of peace, a sense of direction because he'd finally decided to take action. Congratulating himself on this and the fact that he was saving not only Harry but the whole of Cheshire, despite the need to be wary, he fell asleep.

When he woke, Sally was standing in the doorway, white-faced. 'Jools, the police are here. A child is missing. They want to talk to you.'

'Me?' He struggled to keep his eyes open. His head felt full of lead.

'They say it's just routine.' But her face wasn't routine. He rolled off the bed.

There were two of them, a man and a woman. They were sitting at the kitchen table. They weren't wearing uniforms. Sally offered tea but they waved her away.

The woman said, 'Mr Thornton, we're here because a small boy has been missing for several hours – Harry Benson. Do you know him?'

Julian shook his head. 'There aren't many kids round here.'

'He's staying with his grandmother, Doris Glover. Do you know her?' This time they included Sally.

'Is she the lady with the purple hair – she cleans the community centre?' Sally said.

'Yes, so you do know her?'

'Only by sight,' Sally said. 'I didn't know she had a grandson.'

'I don't know her,' Julian said.

'Weren't you in the shop when Mrs Glover came in asking about her grandson?' The man spoke for the first time. His voice was rude, abrasive. Julian looked at them both. It was hard to tell if they were still human or not. If they'd been converted they were doing a good cover-up job but it was best not to trust them to be on the safe side.

'Someone came in,' he said. 'I didn't notice who it was.'

'Can you tell us where you were between four and five this afternoon?' The woman spoke softly but Julian sensed an undertone of menace.

Sally said, 'I was here. We'd just got home. We'd been to Bala for a day out.'

'I went for some milk,' Julian said, 'and I had a bit of a walk, I needed some fresh air.'

'Did you see anyone while you were walking? Anyone who could corroborate that?'

'Only the people in the shop.'

'Why did you go to the shop?' It was the man again, aggressive.

'I told you we were out of milk.' Julian let annoyance into his voice, just to show the arrogant bastard.

'But you went to the shop more than once, didn't you?' It was the woman again. As if he couldn't see their game: her with her soft sickly voice trying to worm things out after the other one had rattled him.

'Yes– yes I did.'

Sally looked at him.

The woman officer looked curiously at him. 'Why did you go back?' Her voice was a velvet trap.

'For some sweets,' he mumbled.

'You bought quite a lot of confectionery, Mr Thornton. Chocolate bars, crisps and those cheap mix sweets, cola bottles, egg-shaped ones.' His voice was hectoring.

The woman officer smiled. 'The kind of sweets children like.' She dropped it like a stone into a pool.

'I – I was hungry. We'd been out all day.' He was conscious of Sally's eyes fixed on him from across the room.

'Hungry?' the man said. Funny how he could put so much disbelief in one word.

'Yes,' Julian said stoutly.

'And when you went walking, Mr Thornton, where did you go?' His stare was impudent, challenging.

'Along the top path, through the nature reserve, towards Gronant,' Julian lied.

'But you saw no one?'

'No.'

'Pity.'

'What time did you get home?' The woman was writing in her notebook.

'It must have been about ten to five,' Sally said. 'I kept looking at the clock because I was waiting for the milk.'

'And you never saw this boy?' She was playing with him, she knew he was lying.

'No.'

The woman closed her notebook. 'That's all for now, Mr Thornton. We may need to see you again. We are interviewing everyone in the neighbourhood.'

Julian nodded. The man got heavily to his feet, giving Julian an I-know-you're-guilty look as he did so.

Julian looked at Sally and saw she was crying. She must still be human and the thought brought great relief. He moved to comfort her.

'It's so awful,' she said, 'to think a child could be taken here.'

In his head, Julian agreed. Was Sally then too aware? Was she also one of the chosen? Was this why they had been brought together?

114

'Try not to upset yourself, Mrs Thornton,' the policewoman said as she got to her feet. 'The boy may simply be lost, have got shut in a shed somewhere, or trapped himself in a ditch. There are search parties out. If he's there, we'll find him.'

'We'll go too, won't we Julian?' Sally said, reaching for her jacket by the back kitchen door.

Clever, clever Sally. 'Of course,' Julian said, getting up as Sally showed them out. He sat down again and listened to the finality of the front door closing behind the officers. His mind was leaping and falling with fear but his terror was overlaid with joy that he was not alone; Sally was there to help him. He'd thought he would have to leave without her, run away with Harry on the train but now a whole new future opened up for the two of them and the boy. They would still have to go of course, they were on to him now and the police were almost certainly part of it. There was no way they would leave it at that, they would be back or at least following him, watching him, waiting for him to lead them to the boy.

The boy was special, he had to be saved for a greater purpose and he, Julian and Sally had been chosen for the task. In the greater picture of things, his love for Sally was probably just a tiny pixel. Maybe this was an opportunity for him to show his mettle; maybe there was some greater role earmarked for him in the salvation of mankind and this was just a test.

They'd have to go now, dodge the police. Maybe he could throw them off the scent while Sally collected the boy. And now she was on his side, they could take her car, leave it somewhere it would take them a couple of days to find it and get the late train to Chester – then what? He wouldn't worry about that, there would be a sign to show him what to do. The important thing was to get away.

The sound of Sally's returning footsteps broke into his thoughts. She closed the kitchen door and leaned against it. Her eyes were cold as a lizard's. He barely recognised her as his own beloved Sally.

'Julian, you never eat sweets,' she said.

Losing Adrian

'Why don't you come up and stay for a few days?'
Lally sounded anxious, but then she always did.

'What for?' Milly Pink shuffled the evening
newspaper delivery on the shop counter. Trust her sister
to ring and start mithering her when she was busy. Any
minute now the schoolkids would be in, supposedly
buying sweets. You needed eyes in the back of your
head. Thankfully, there weren't many kids in Plotlands,
once the tourist season was over; most of them
belonged to the Dolans, tinkers the lot of them. When
they all came in together they were like a flock of
starlings and her eyes weren't as sharp as they used to
be.

'Give you a break, you're not getting any younger,'
Lally's voice broke in on her thoughts.

'Don't talk wet,' Milly shifted the phone between
her ear and her neck, while she tried to count out copies
of the Evening Leader. Lally's voice droned like a
mosquito while she struggled to remember how many
copies the delivery boy needed. Damn her sister, now
she'd have to look in the order book again. 'I don't
need a break,' she snapped, 'and I can't leave the shop
anyhow.'

'They think I'm going senile,' she thought angrily,
once she'd fobbed Lally off yet again. She was always
ringing up lately, inviting her up for this or that event:
family birthdays, christenings. Why on earth would she
want to go up there to stay with Lally, listen to her
bragging about her kids' successful lives, put up with

117

her snivelling grandchildren? For a moment she thought of Adrian but she stopped herself and concentrated on filling the paperboy's bag, making sure the addresses were pencilled on each paper.

It was like putting on your corset, dealing with grief. People expected you to do it, appear as if everything was normal again. It made them uncomfortable if you didn't, like Lally felt uncomfortable, like she ought to help in some way when Milly'd made it perfectly clear that she didn't need any help. But Lally had always been the protective older sister, from back in the old days, when they'd first come to Plotlands after the war.

Milly couldn't remember that because she'd only been a year old. She had no memory of the wooden bungalow where they'd first lived, the one Lally always went on about, telling everybody what fun they'd had living right down on the beach. Milly let her pencil fall as she recalled the cottage of her childhood. Her father had built it of bricks, on a plot further up near the road that he'd saved up for several years to buy. That must have been in the late 1940s or early 50s. She remembered how it stood out among the wooden sheds and old buses other families lived in.

Even so there had been no running water, no electricity. Her mother had cooked on a primus stove and the rooms were lit by paraffin lamps. Milly remembered trailing behind Lally to the stand pipes on the main road for water, several times a day sometimes; remembered crying at having to carry the heavy bucket back and Lally smacking her round the head and telling her to stop being mardy. Milly remembered it as it was, not through Lally's rose-tinted glasses but it was true there were happy memories too and Milly was rooted, drawn back to Plotlands when she and George married,

118

after a long stint of working at various holiday camps across Wales.

The shop bell went and she started, orienting herself as the Dolan kids rushed in, followed by a gaggle that'd got off the bus with them, all screeching and rushing around, sticky fingers everywhere. She did her best to guard the chocolate display, thankfully some of their mothers came in and marshalled a semblance of order and then they got to gossiping about the doolally chap who'd kidnapped Doris Glover's grandson. Milly's ears pricked up when Bridie Dolan said the wife had put the house up for sale after he'd been put in the hospital, not just the ordinary hospital but one of those locked ones where they can't get out. Another empty house –if things went on like this, Plotlands would be a ghost town before long. Doris Glover had told her the week before that she'd heard a rumour that someone had applied to build new houses at Plotlands but Milly hadn't taken any notice. Why would people want to build new houses when there were so many of the old ones standing empty?

She quite forgot about Lally and her pestering until she was in her bed that night. Bedtime was always full of dangerous memories – of George's blocky body lying warm next to her. She could never get used to that cold space, even though it was thirteen years since he'd died, when Adrian was only a tiny boy. Then came memories of Adrian – how she used to bring him into the bed, as a baby, when he wouldn't sleep.

They'd still been living in the cottage then, Mum and Dad both dead and Lally married to a Scouser and living in Walton Vale in Liverpool. But then, change was coming to Plotlands as inevitably as the shifting sand dunes were changing the landscape. People were leaving, the old homesteads and neat little gardens

119

abandoned here and there as the sea receded still further and the beach elongated into a marshy mess. Sometimes the sea flooded up invading occupied and empty property without distinction. Milly and the rest of the residents were used to this and also to the sand forever moving and blowing. It was part of their daily routine to keep the sand away from their doors but it had full sway on the empty properties so that it soon came up to the windowledges of the derelict homes. It hadn't always been like that but the coastline was changing; folks said it was something to do with the building of sea defences and groynes further along the headland and they shook their heads and made plans to move away, into council houses in Rhyl and Prestatyn with hot water and lots of sockets for electric gadgets.

George had wanted to move too but Milly had hung on because the house was hers and her father had built it and she couldn't bear to see it swallowed up by the sand and the sea but then George had been killed on the building site where he was working and she was left alone with a small baby, at the mercy of the forces of nature.

Lally had pushed her to move to Liverpool, saying, 'After all, it's where our family came from,' but Plotlands had been Milly's life, it was woven into her being. The shop had come up like a heaven sent opportunity at the same time as the compensation money for George's death. It was on the main road, safely away from the beach; it had living accommodation over it and all mod cons for the time. It had been a safe haven for bringing up Adrian. She could almost see him: the way his tiny fist would curl round her finger, his little fluff of hair, soft brown against the pillow and the clear gaze of those blue eyes as if he was wondering who – or what – she was.

It seemed as if she was all that existed in the world for him as she watched him, drowning in the delicious slackness of his mouth, so delicate as he relaxed into sleep, moist bubbles at the corners of his lips. All that care, all those years watching him grow, just to end so suddenly, without even a goodbye…

'Stop it, stop it,' she told herself as she tossed, sleepless, the image of Lally yammering down the phone now tormenting her. Why couldn't she leave her alone?

The next day was fine but cold. She had a nice trip on the bus to Prestatyn but she wanted to get home in time for Adrian's tea. It wasn't right, keeping a baby out after dark and it got dark just after four, these winter afternoons. Having the pram meant she had to walk so it was almost dark anyway by the time she got back. Luckily the shop was closed for half-day on Wednesdays in winter so no one was expecting her to be on hand till six, when she would open up for people who needed the evening paper or a pint of milk. By that time, Adrian would be fed and tucked up in bed.

The light was starting to fade as she came along the path from Gronant, the dunes humping beside her as she passed. The lighthouse still stood in proud isolation on the beach, but the pretty garden that had once surrounded it and the prefabs that had straggled nearby were long gone.

Milly thought of the remains of those buildings and gardens still there under her feet buried beneath years of sand. Hard to think such a thing could happen, she thought as she passed the chimney stack of the house where the McLaren family had lived, still sticking up

121

out of a small dune. She'd used to play with the McLaren girls, Dawn and Lavinia and she wondered where they were now, women with families of their own no doubt. She stopped by the plum tree that had stood in Mrs Manger's garden and thought of the childhood games they had played there but Adrian started to grizzle and she reminded herself that he needed his tea.

She made his favourite, soft-boiled egg and ate the toast herself; he wasn't quite old enough for soldiers yet. She gave him a bath and got a fresh pack of nappies from the shop stock. He giggled and cooed at her, just getting to that lovely age when he recognised her and had learnt to show happiness. Luckily there was a bottle in the pram so she warmed him some milk and he took it eagerly as he always did.

'You make me happy too, darling,' she said, tucking him in and thinking he was getting too big to sleep in the wooden drawer she used for his bed. He needed some new clothes too. Tomorrow, she thought, with a burst of energy, she would take him into Rhyl on the bus and get him some new things.

By the time he'd gone to sleep, Milly felt really tired so she sat down with a cup of tea to watch the early news on Channel 5 before opening the shop. The news was all about wars and fighting in dusty places full of wrecked buildings and it made her feel uncomfortable, although it was nothing to do with her, was it? She tried to bring back the pleasant memories of her childhood but her earlier happy mood evaded her.

She switched channels to *Flog It* but a memory was stirring in her brain, a flag-draped coffin floating through the streets of some town – something she'd seen on the news? She struggled for the name of it but it was lost. There were people lining the streets, throwing flowers. A tear rolled from her eye but she had no idea why. The shop bell jangled and she jerked up, looking at the mantel clock. Six o'clock. Where had she been?

'You're late opening tonight,' the customer said. 'Are you okay? You look a bit peaky.'

'I'm fine,' Milly snapped, shaking her head to drive the image of that coffin out of her mind. 'What can I get you?' She looked up at the woman, trying to place her. Perhaps she was a winter visitor, though they were unusual. Was she a hiker? She peered over the counter at the woman's legs but she was wearing ordinary white trainers, none too clean either. 'Are you staying local?' she asked, fetching the half-bottle of gin the woman asked for.

'What d'ye mean?' the woman stared at her and Milly's mind cleared as she recognised Bridie Dolan. 'Oh, silly me,' she giggled, 'it's the light in here and my eyes aren't so good without my glasses.' She lifted her glasses on the chain round her neck and fitted them on as she pulled Bridie's regular copy of *People's Friend* from the orders under the counter.

Bridie gave her a funny look but made no comment. 'I'd better be having some more milk,' she said, reaching into the cooler, 'the kids have drunk up the whole lot, the greedy eejits. Whose is the pram then?' she asked, plonking the milk down on the counter and getting out her huge plastic purse.

'Pram?' Milly followed her gaze. Suddenly she remembered Adrian, sleeping sweetly in the bedroom. He was such a good baby.

'Your sister down, is she? Brought one of her grandchildren?' Bridie's eyes were brightly curious.

'Two-seventy-five, please.' Milly wasn't going to put her right; it was none of her business, nosy cow.

123

'Children are a blessing, aren't they?' Bridie said, 'Although at times it doesn't feel like it, with them all screeching and demanding.' She stopped suddenly and bit her lip. 'I'm sorry, I didn't mean…'

She laid a hand on Milly's arm before Milly could pull it away. 'May Holy Mother bring you blessings – I pray every night.'

Milly didn't answer. She stood stone-faced as Bridie left in a fluster, pushing her change hurriedly in the big purse.

It was almost nine before she could shut up the shop with people coming in all the time for bits and bobs. Her last customer was Nolly Perkins, a gangly teenager who she suspected of secreting her goods in the pockets and folds of his hoodie, but whom she never managed to catch.

'Wootton Bassett,' she said suddenly as she served him a packet of Carlton King Size.

'Yer what?' Nolly said, shaking his head as he went out as if to say, 'Old people today.'

Milly bolted the door after him gratefully. She was bone-tired and almost fell over the pram which she'd moved behind the backroom door after Bridie's questions. Adrian woke up and began to cry so she changed him and gave him his last feed before they both settled down for the night.

'If only George hadn't taken that job in Flint,' she thought, feeling that cold space again on his side of the bed. He wouldn't have fallen off the scaffolding and she and Adrian wouldn't be all alone. Men in her family seemed prone to dangerous jobs. Her father had injured his back in a fall while working on Liverpool docks before they came to Plotlands and he'd suffered pain the rest of his relatively short life. The image of that coffin came again, forming ghostly in her mind, but she pushed it away, turned on her bedside lamp and immersed herself in *Woman's Weekly* till she fell asleep.

She shut the shop at ten the next morning after the newspapers were sorted and people had their early morning sweets, bread and milk. They would all just have to manage till she got back. She set the card in the glass panel of the door, with its clock fingers at one. That should give her plenty of time.

She caught the bus, carrying Adrian, well wrapped up. She'd forgotten how heavy he was. He was a bit grizzly but she kept him quiet with a lollipop and when she got to Rhyl, the first thing she bought was a pushchair, the kind you could fold up on the bus. It seemed a lot of money but he was getting to the age where she would get plenty of use out of it.

She walked along the prom, pushing Adrian while she tried to remember the other things she needed to buy. A proper cot, of course, but that would have to be delivered and some more bottles.She bought some nice clothes in the charity shops, after all he wouldn't be in them long, babies grew so quickly. There were such lovely things for them nowadays.

She remembered how few clothes she'd had as a child and nearly all home-made or second-hand. Her mother used to tell a story of how the Air Force used the Plotlands beach for target practice. They would lay out cotton sheets in the shape of crosses and once the practice was over the Plotlands women would run out and filch the sheets and cut them up for clothes and bedding. Milly fingered the fleecy blankets and coloured babygros but she was back on the Plotlands beach with Lally picking up spent shell cases to polish up and sell to the holidaymakers at the camp as candleholders, their skirts whipping in the sea breeze, sand stinging their legs. They were laughing, they were always laughing.

All of a sudden it began to get quite dark and Adrian kept grizzling and crying so she ducked into a café and ordered two plates of chips and a pot of tea.

'He's a bit young for chips, isn't he?' said the waitress, looking doubtfully at Adrian.

'He's very advanced for his age,' said Milly but Adrian wouldn't eat the chips at all. He turned red in the face and bawled. Milly thought maybe he needed changing.

'Hey, you can't do that in here,' the waitress rushed over. 'Take him in the loo.'

Adrian was still howling when Milly brought him back and she realised she'd forgotten his bottle so she dipped her fingers in her tea and let him suck them.

The waitress was whispering to someone in the kitchen doorway, then she disappeared into the back. 'Silly cow,' Milly thought, smiling at Adrian who was quiet now, sucking peacefully on her finger. She finished her tea and was halfway to the bus stop when she remembered she'd left the café without paying and turned back. There was something else she'd forgotten but it wouldn't come to her, until she came in sight of the café and saw the police car outside. Adrian – she'd left him behind. He'd fallen asleep in the pushchair, exhausted with crying and she'd put the buggy in the corner while she finished her lunch. How could she have forgotten him?

As she approached, she could see, through the window, a woman police constable carrying Adrian and chucking him under the chin. He was crying again, she could hear him from outside. A male constable was talking to the waitress and writing things down.

'– and she went off without paying,' the waitress was saying as Milly rushed into the café.

'I don't know what they're thinking of, putting me in here,' Milly said to Lally, 'the place is full of loonies.'

'Mil..' Lally began but Milly wasn't having any of her nonsense.

'And there wasn't any need for you to come running down here. I'll be going home in a day or so. I'm only here for a rest, that's what they said, I needed a rest.'

'It's not that simple, Mil,' Lally said. She reached out and took Milly's hands, stopped them twisting in her lap. Milly looked up, surprised, as Lally stroked the backs of her fingers. She and Lally hadn't touched for years and years, not since they were teenagers laughing over clothes and boys together in the cottage on the beach. She just wanted to go home there now and she opened her mouth to tell Lally but then she remembered it wasn't there any more and they were all dead, Mum and Dad and George and….

She looked at Lally's hands, spotted and wrinkled now, but still soft. That soft touch made her want to weep and Lally's face blurred as tears prickled. She pulled her hand away and rubbed at her eyes.

How old Lally had got, she thought, looking at her face when her vision had cleared. Where had all that time gone? It didn't seem five minutes since they'd played together all through the long summer holidays. Sometimes for fun, she and Lally had been allowed to camp in a tent in the farm field at the top end of the Plotlands road. They'd bought comics at the little post office; now it was the camp shop at the Beach Caravan

127

Park. Then the park had been the Beach Holiday Park full of little wooden chalets. They'd eventually been replaced by shiny caravans that had modern conveniences but lacked the quaint attractiveness of the old huts. She remembered how she'd been scared of the moths that came in the tent at night and Lally –

'Mil…' Lally broke in on her thoughts. 'You can't just go home, not yet anyhow.'

'But I'm fine,' Milly said. 'I've had a good sleep and I'm rested now. The food in here is awful and besides I need to get back to the shop. I'll miss the last train.'

'Milly the train station closed in 1964. Don't you remember?' Lally sighed. 'Sonia's looking after the shop. You're not to worry about the shop.'

'Sonia!' Milly cried. 'What does Sonia know about running the shop?' The thought of Lally's daughter poking around in her shop made her jump to her feet. 'I'm getting my coat.' She looked around but couldn't see any sign of her belongings. 'What happened to my shopping?' She opened the cupboard next to her bed but there was nothing in it except a toilet bag and a nightie she'd never seen before. 'What do you mean, the station's closed?'

'I took it home for you,' Lally said. 'All those baby clothes. What were you thinking?'

'Adrian needed new things,' Milly said. She knew something was wrong but what was it? She kept her eyes away from Lally's stare and picked at her skirt.

'Adrian's dead, Milly,' Lally said. 'Don't you remember the funeral, all the army people who came – and the medal, Adrian's medal? You put it in your sideboard.'

'I know that,' Milly shouted. 'Of course I remember,' but she felt very frightened. 'I was just

128

remembering,' she whispered, 'how he was when he was little – and the things in the shops were so pretty.'

'You took someone else's baby,' Lally said. 'Don't you remember? The baby was outside the chip shop in Prestatyn. His mum had only popped inside for a sausage dinner.'

'Me?' Milly was astonished. 'Why would I ever do a thing like that? How could you think something like that about me?'

Lally sighed. She looked terribly tired – and aged. 'She looks much older than me,' Milly thought, 'even though she's three years younger. That's what comes of telling lies.'

'Mil…' Lally reached out to her but Milly pulled away, got up and stalked to the other side of the bed.

'Go away,' she said, turning her back and staring out of the window. 'I don't want to talk to you.'

After Lally had gone, she lay on her bed and slept for a while and when she woke up she thought it had all been a dream because, ever since Adrian died she had dreamed of him as a baby, a little boy, growing up into a teenager. She'd longed for sleep at night to take her back to those times they'd had together. But if it had been a dream, then why was she in this place?

She'd been thirty when she'd come back to Plotlands for good, when all the things she'd given up hope on suddenly came true. She'd thought she would never get married, not this late, with Lally already married five years with two kids. Janice was already at nursery school and Sonia was starting to toddle. And when the miracle did happen, when she met George, she thought she'd never have a child as the years of her marriage went by and she burned under Lally's constant showing off the results of her fertility. Janice had been born suspiciously early, seven months to the day from Lally and Mark's wedding and Sonia came not long after, a barely decent interval between the two.

But then it had happened. She hadn't dared breathe a word until the doctor confirmed it and even then she didn't believe it, not really, not until her belly started to swell and she felt that first flutter.

They'd teased her, Lally and her husband, for taking up with a taff and a Chapel man at that, but George wasn't really religious at all; he'd just been brought up strict and that did no one any harm, did it? She hadn't had much choice and no one else had asked her to marry them, had they? It was like Lally expected her to be an old maid, babysitting her girls and providing her family with a holiday each summer. Milly'd taken over the cottage when Mum had passed on six months after the cancer took Dad but she hadn't really lived there much, she'd always worked away.

Once she'd married things were different. She did her best to smarten the place up, her time taken up with learning about love and sex and playing house. It wasn't ideal but they couldn't afford anything else. Even though it was shabby, it was clean and warm, private, sitting on its own big plot that was perfect for a child to play in. It was pretty in summer, hedged with pink hydrangeas and when she looked out of its windows she pictured herself pushing a pram along the beach path. That's what a baby needed, fresh air and room to grow. And she had such memories. Even now, every time she walked to Gronant, she saw in her mind's eye all the Plotlands kids playing Cowboys and Indians among the dunes, fuelled by sessions at Prestatyn's Scala cinema's Saturday morning pictures.

It had been the right decision. Oh, it was bleak and cold in winter, and isolated – a long walk to the main road to catch a bus to Prestatyn or Flint before they'd put a bus stop on the Plotlands road but then George got a little car. By then she'd fallen in love with the place all over again: the open views and the keen air coming in from the distant sea; the cries of seabirds feeding on the marsh, the bare colours of winter and the bright holiday atmosphere in summer.

She liked the tourist season, when people came like flocks of exotic birds, endless streams arriving and leaving. Even the people who lived here seemed to come and go, there was always someone new, some hurried departure, some gossip and scandal. Yet Plotlands people were forgiving, once the initial curiosity had died down. She felt at home there, people rubbed along together, lived and let live.

She hadn't thought twice about it when the shop came up after George died. She had the money and she had to make a living somehow for herself and Adrian. There'd been a twinge of regret for leaving the old place but she had to move with the times and she wanted all the modern things that Adrian deserved and everybody else was taking for granted: a washing machine, wall to wall carpets, a television…

Now they wanted to winkle her out of her little shop. As if she could just leave home after all these years. That was what Lally wanted, all that asking her to go and stay with her and now she'd heard her muttering to the social worker. But she couldn't leave. She had to keep the place for Adrian to come home to, when he came out of the army.

Pride swelled her whole body; her boy, so big and strong. She hadn't wanted him to join up but he'd been determined. 'There's nothing for me here, Mum. I want

131

to see the world.' What more world is there than here? she'd wanted to say; a world that had kept her enthralled for all these years. Even now it filled her with wonder: marvellous dawns and dusks and wide, wide skies. She pictured the sea that waved on the Plotlands beach, spreading, spreading all around the world to all those foreign shores where Adrian had gone, but of course, he couldn't see that, young people's visions are narrow. It was enough to see him happy, strong and tanned and at ease in his uniform with his mates in the photos lined up on her mantelpiece.

Something dark blossomed in her mind and she moved uneasily on the bed and opened her eyes. The other people in the ward were all gathered round a long table; shapeless, nameless figures, eating. A nurse stood at the side of her bed. No uniform – how silly. You wouldn't know she was a nurse except for the badge she wore. What kind of nursing was that? Money saving, Milly supposed, it was all these places thought about nowadays. They'd save more by letting perfectly healthy people like herself go home.

'Won't you come and have some tea, Milly?' the nurse said, 'it's chicken curry.'

'I don't like curry,' Milly said. She turned her face to the wall and wished she was at home with her telly and a tin of tomato soup for her supper.

Lally was muttering with the social worker again. Milly thought she must have been asleep and missed her arrival. Snatches of the conversation caught on her ear – 'been there donkeys' years' – 'it'll kill her'….

Lally's voice, always loud and sharp, came out as a stage whisper, frighteningly false. The social worker's voice was full of sweet menace, even though Milly could only hear occasional actual words......"not well enough".........."not safe'...

Terror washed through her as she realised what they were up to; it was all for Sonia. They were plotting together, Lally and that snobby girl (how could a girl so young be entrusted with making decisions about people's lives?). Sonia was already installed in the shop, no doubt rooting among Milly's things and upsetting all the stock. It was obvious – Lally wanted the shop, wanted Sonia to have the shop; she'd never been able to get a proper job and Lally often said she'd like to get her away from that no-good man she kept going back to.

Milly's tongue stuck to the roof of her mouth with fright. They wanted to keep her in here, or put her in a home, somewhere where she'd never get out, where she'd droop and die like flowers on a grave, with no one to care.

If only Adrian would come home, he'd put a stop to their wiles but Adrian was thousands of miles away and she didn't know when his next leave was due. It seemed such a long time since she'd seen him. Anyway, she couldn't just sit and wait. Once they'd got control of the shop she wouldn't be able to stop them – there was some legal thing, possession is nine points of something...

She got out of bed quietly. Lally and the social worker were too engrossed in their plotting to notice. There wasn't time to look for her coat and shoes; they'd obviously hidden them to keep her prisoner here. The ward was quiet; most of them were in the big room at the bottom where some kind of singing was going on.

She had to get past the nurses' station but there was only one girl on there and she was on the phone. She looked up as Milly passed but Milly smiled innocently and shuffled towards the toilet, only changing tack at the last minute when the nurse looked down and started riffling through some notes as she talked into the phone.

Milly didn't know where she was but a bus passed her with RHYL marked on the front so she thought she must be going the right way and when she came to a bus stop she would stop and wait. But then she realised she hadn't got her handbag with her bus pass inside and to her surprise, she started to cry, something she'd rarely done since Adrian… She was feeling cold too, without her coat and cold from the ground bit through her slippers and rose up her bare legs. There was a bit of a wind blowing up and spots of rain began to blow in her face.

Someone pulled up in a car and asked if she was all right and if she wanted a lift. Somehow all the houses had disappeared and there were only fields on both sides of the road and a distant view of an unfamiliar sea. The driver seemed a nice young lady so Milly got in and told her she was going home to Plotlands and the lady said she knew it well and sometimes went there with her children for a day out so Milly told her about the shop and about Adrian. She got so lost in Adrian's childhood that she was surprised when the car suddenly stopped and she found that the lady hadn't brought her to Plotlands but to the police station in Rhyl.

The police were very nice and polite and they gave her a cup of tea and some digestive biscuits but they wouldn't listen to what she told them and the next thing she knew she was back at the hospital where the nurses told her off as if she was a naughty child. Lally kept asking what she was thinking of and then someone gave her an injection and she went to sleep and when she woke up it was night and Lally was gone.

The next morning the social worker came to see Milly but Lally wasn't with her. Milly set her face against her but she couldn't close her ears. She had a soft voice, this social worker, but it said terrible things, pretending all the time, pretending to be kind, to be doing her job for Milly's benefit. She murmured things like, 'best solution' and, 'what's best for you.' All the time Milly kept remembering what she'd really been saying to Lally the day before: 'can't look after herself'..."will only get worse'... and so on. Milly thought how she'd had to look after herself all her life. These young girls had no idea how had life had been in the fifties and sixties.

It takes a pretender to recognise pretence and the social worker's eyes bored into Milly letting her know that she could see past the front Milly was putting up, of being calm, rational and agreeable. Her gaze said she saw how Milly hoped the social worker would realise she was mistaken and would let her go home, when really she wanted to jump on her and claw her lying eyes out.

'Your sister's happy to have you live with her...' the woman paused as Milly recoiled involuntarily, 'but she feels that you wouldn't be happy with that. She thinks you wouldn't want to leave your home – and the shop.'

'You won't remember the winter of 1963,' Milly said to the social worker who stared at her in surprise. Of course she wasn't even born then, Milly thought, sinking into her recollection of the snow, topping the hedges and making the Plotlands road disappear. Mr Metcalf's car had been totally submerged and everyone had got together to dig it out, not that he could drive it as the road stayed under the drifts for days at a time until snow ploughs came and the whole community had to keep turning out with shovels just so they could get to work. Lally had still been at home then. She and Milly, forgetting they were grown up young ladies now, had shrieked their way down the snowy dunes on tin trays with all the younger kids. It was the following summer Lally got married and Milly went away to work at the Butlin's camp in Pwlheli and life changed after that.

She struggled back to the present. The social worker was looking at her with a question in her eyes. She'd said something about staying in the shop? Milly didn't dare speak. She was instantly flooded with hope and, before she could stop them, the damned tears ran down her face again.

'It's all right,' the social worker took her hand, stroked it gently, which made Milly cry all the more. 'What we thought,' she hesitated, 'your sister suggested – her daughter Sonia could stay with you, help you with the shop. Would you like that?' She waited, letting her suggestion sink in. Her smiling face said that she was sure Milly would be pleased with this solution.

She might as well have smacked her in the face. Milly's body and her hopes sank in the unaccommodating hospital chair. Oh, clever, clever Lally and Sonia. There was no way Milly could get out of this, the alternative would be…

She shuddered.

'I can make the arrangements quite soon,' the social worker said briskly. 'You could possibly be home this evening – tomorrow at the latest.'

Carrot to catch the donkey, thought Milly but the thought of going home to her shop and her customers, her whole familiar life and landscape, filled her with longing so that being fooled by the social worker, Lally and Sonia hardly seemed to matter.

She sat up straight and smiled and the social worker smiled and looked relieved. 'I'll go and talk to the ward manager then?' She raised her eyebrows.

Milly nodded. She would go home and be pleasant to everyone, especially Sonia. It would only be for a little while anyway – just till Adrian came...

That's What I Want

Nolly Perkins scuffed through the dead leaves and winter litter clogging the narrow pavement. He hunched his shoulders to ward off the wind that blew in from the sea and bit into his thin jacket. It was already starting to go dark, although it was barely four o'clock. Fifteen minutes to hang around waiting for Tombo, if he turned up at all that was.

The chippy was open, an island of light and warmth; delicious smells wafted out. Nolly's mouth watered but he'd spent the last of his own money on a packet of fags and what he had in his pocket belonged to Tombo. He couldn't go and keep warm in the discount store across the road either, not since they'd caught him lifting six jars of their shit coffee. Everything else was closed up for the winter.

Nolly walked past the shuttered windows of the amusement arcades and the ice-cream parlour to the car park of the Smuggler's Rest, where he was supposed to meet Tombo. He tried to shelter from the wind among the bushes that were planted round the borders of the tarmacked space. Some old bat in an anorak came past leading a bedraggled Yorkshire terrier that perked up and yapped when it saw Nolly. She stared at him like she thought he was a peeping tom so Nolly came out of the bushes, lit a cigarette, gave her a dirty look and walked up and down.

At last came the lights of Tombo's car. Nolly knew it was him by the loud thump of bass overriding the engine. He felt in his jacket pocket to make sure the money was still there.

'Nol?' Tombo rolled down his window and heat rushed into Nolly's face as he bent to the car. Tombo's hand was already out for the money. The window rolled up again while Tombo riffled through the notes for ages. Probably can't count, Nolly thought, shifting from one foot to the other to keep warm.

Two heavies were squashed in the back seat. Nolly sensed their bulk, even though all he could make out were their eyes, cold with threat. Wankers, he thought. You'd think with all the business he did with them, Tombo would at least invite him to sit in the warm car.

As he was thinking this, the window opened again and a hand held out a package. Nolly took it and stowed it in his jacket pocket.

'Payday's Friday,' Tombo said. 'Ring me.' The window was still rolling up as the car skidded backwards and then shot out of the car park.

'Twats!' Nolly muttered to himself but now he was happy; he had the stuff and he could go home and get warm. On the way back he allowed himself to stop off at Milly Pink's back garden.

Nolly's nan was taking a casserole out of the oven when he walked in the back kitchen.

'You look frozen half to death, Norman. Where've you been? We've been waiting supper for you. Come and sit down and get warm.' She fussed round him, unzipping at his jacket.

Nolly fended her off, mindful of the contents of his pockets. 'Won't be a sec Nan, just need to wash my hands.' He scooted upstairs to his room and hid the package in the sports bag in his wardrobe. He went into the bathroom and ran the tap then came back down.

He sat down at the table; the heat of the kitchen was wonderful after being out so long in the cold and he relaxed back in the chair, spreading his legs.

Nolly's granddad looked up from the *Evening Leader*, his mouth turned down as usual.

'You need a good winter coat,' his nan said, laying knives and forks. 'Maybe Santa will bring you one for Christmas.'

'He wants to get a bloody job, instead of hanging round like a tart.' Nolly's granddad growled.

'Ain't no jobs,' Nolly muttered. It was the same stupid exchange that went on every night. If he hadn't been so cold and hungry, he'd have gone straight up to his room, out of their way; stupid old crumblies.

'Nineteen and never done a proper day's work,' Nolly's granddad shook the paper and clicked his teeth.

'He is trying, aren't you Norman?' His nan tried to ruffle his hair but Nolly ducked away. He bent over his plate and began to shovel the food in as fast as he could, without looking up at his nan's pity. He didn't have to look at his granddad's miserable gob but he couldn't avoid hearing his snort of disgust.

'So what you do today? How many jobs you try for today, this week, this month?' He was in full flow now, intent on needling him and despite himself, Nolly rose to the bait.

'There's nothing in this dump. Anyway, I'll be going home at Christmas.'

'Ha!' his granddad snorted. '*She* doesn't want you. Why do you think she dumped you here on us?'

Nolly thought of the bitter greens the disciples ate at the last supper, one of the few images that had stuck in his mind from his mother's religious rantings. When he

141

was small, he used to think his granddad had eaten too many of them. Since then, Nolly never liked to eat anything green.

'Ssh now,' Nolly's nan pulled a shocked face at her husband. 'It's not that she don't want him; she can't cope, you know that Don. She always was fragile.'

'Fragile my arse,' Nolly's granddad said. 'It's him,' he glared at Nolly. 'All that religious claptrap hasn't helped him has it? Look at him. Who could cope with him?' He wagged a finger at Nolly. 'You're heading for jail, you are mate and good riddance to you. Don't think I don't know what you get up to.'

Nolly thought of the package in the wardrobe. He didn't look up; if he did, his granddad would see not only guilt but the murderous rage he felt towards him at that moment. He scraped the last bit of food from his plate, clattered his knife and fork down, got up and went out of the room without a word. As he started to climb the stairs to his room, he heard his nan say, 'You shouldn't say things like that. It was those city boys, running around in gangs, a bad influence on him. He's been a good boy since he's been here.'

It didn't take Nolly long to cut the block into deals, naturally scraping a bit off here and there for himself. He licked his lips in anticipation as he worked, then made long joint with a sigh of pleasure. It was heaven to be quiet in his room, his belly full, his mind softening and opening to the night as the smoke in his lungs transferred the drug to his bloodstream. Comfort oozed through him and the night air wrapped him like fleece. He could barely feel the cold as he sat at the open window, puffing out his acrid breath. His nan was too stupid to notice the smoke or the smell but he wasn't so sure about his granddad. After all, he'd been to sea in his youth. Nolly was sick of hearing him going on about how he'd seen the world, and how he'd worked on Flint docks for many a year before he retired.

There was yet another pleasure to complete the evening. He felt in his jacket pocket for the knickers he'd lifted from Milly Pink's washing line. Since Sonia had come to live there, the washing line had borne better fruit than Milly's baggy old pants. He stroked the soft, silky fabric, put it to his nose and smelled the clean, detergent-and-fresh-air smell. When he put them on, he thought he would come in them, right there and then, but he managed to hold back. He wrapped himself in his duvet, sat up to the window and lit up another joint.

Nolly sat in the warm fug of the Saracen on Rhyl promenade, smiling with the satisfaction of a successful night. The evening was made even rosier by the occasional gift of a spliff from a grateful client.

He felt his pockets, heavy with notes and grinned. He'd offloaded most of the gear but still had some left. He figured an hour or so at Jakes night club and he'd be able to go home, job done. He'd found a red basque on a washing line at the back of the Plotlands holiday camp that afternoon and he was eager to try it on. Just time for a slash before the pub closed and then he'd get off to the club.

The toilets were empty when he went in but almost as soon as he'd unzipped, the door opened and three strangers came in. Nolly looked at their false smiles in the harshly reflected light of the washroom mirror and his heart faltered. 'They just want some gear,' he told himself but his piss wavered, trickled onto his jeans and shoes.

'Got anything on you?' one said; bulging muscles swelled out of his white tee shirt. Nolly watched as the third carefully closed the washroom door and lodged his bulk behind it.

'What do you mean?' Nolly tried to sound aggressive but the words came out in a whine. His thoughts whirled uselessly. They might be fuzz but they didn't look like fuzz; they looked and sounded like Irish travellers, mean ones.

'What we got here?' one said, coming up close to Nolly and peering at the flash of pink satin that protruded from Nolly's fly, making a little nest around the base of his penis. They all started to laugh and the two not guarding the door shoved and jostled Nolly as he tried desperately to zip himself up. They pulled his jeans down to howls of laughter. 'Look at the hairy arse on him,' one guffawed as Nolly's rear was exposed in all its pink satin glory.

A kick to the back of his legs sent him sprawling on the floor, his legs tangling in his jeans and the reek of stale urine up his nostrils. More kicks followed to his head and body with an accompaniment of curses. A great fist ripped the pink panties from his buttocks and Nolly began to beg through bleeding lips.

'Shut up fucking nancy boy,' someone said and then he heard them unzipping and knew what was coming next. He couldn't think, couldn't hope. Filled with terror, he tried to withdraw somewhere inside himself where they wouldn't reach him as he waited for the worst to happen. It was a relief when something warm and wet splattered on his face and body. When he heard their raucous shouts and laughter dying away, the sound of their boots fading as the door slammed behind them, he couldn't believe his luck. Sonia's pink panties lay on the floor, ruined.

The gear was gone, of course, and so was Tombo's money. The emptiness of his pockets matched that in his brain as it boggled at the thought of what would happen next. Luckily his nan and granddad had gone to bed by the time he picked himself up and crawled home.

He got into bed, the thought of Tombo weighing him down like a monster on his chest trying to steal his soul. It was Saturday night. He had to find £800 by Friday. He couldn't even ring Tombo and try to explain. They'd taken his phone as well, of course and he'd no money to buy another. His teeth chattered. He didn't even have a joint to comfort himself with. The red basque was hidden under his mattress but it was the last thing he wanted. Right now all he could think was that he had less than six days to live.

Maybe his nan and granddad would lend him the money. A light flared briefly in his mind but then faded. There was no way his granddad would let Nolly raid his savings and Nolly knew all his money was tucked up in bank deposits and such because his granddad was always clucking over boring interest rates in the papers.

But his nan might be another matter. Anything she had she would squirrel away somewhere in the house. She was like a lot of old people; didn't trust banks, didn't want anyone to know what they'd got. Nolly'd seen on telly how they were always getting robbed by worthless lowlifes coming round and pretending to fix loose slates on the roof or leaky pipes.

Oh so quietly, he tiptoed downstairs and gently rummaged through the kitchen cupboards. He found

£50 in an empty coffee tin but nothing else. The clock on the mantelpiece in the living room was his next destination, where his nan kept old bills and letters.

The search yielded another £20 tucked in a life insurance paying in book. Nolly thought for a moment of mugging the collector when he came round on Thursday evening but he was a big, burly bloke and Nolly didn't fancy his chances.

Anger and despair made him careless. He tossed the flimsy envelopes and bits of paper in the air, then realising it would give the game away, started to pick them up and put them back. Among them was a lottery ticket, three weeks old. That's how stupid his nan was, she could have won a million and she wouldn't even know.

He pocketed the ticket and the £70 and went upstairs to pack his sports bag with a change of clothes. There was nothing for it but to do a runner, somewhere where Tombo wouldn't find him. He picked over his lingerie collection. There was no way he could take it all with him. He selected the best pieces, including the red basque, then took the rest out and dumped it in next door's wheelie bin. Coming back, he zipped up the bag and lay down on his bed to wait for the dawn.

Before the light stole in, he dropped into a dozing dream where his mother stood over him reciting the Ten Commandments. She was wearing the red basque and long black boots and when she got to 'Thou shalt not steal,' she slashed at his legs with the cane in her hand.

He was out of the house before his grandparents stirred and he walked to Prestatyn to save the bus fare. He stopped at a newsagent's near the bus station and adrenaline raced through his body as he handed the lottery ticket over. 'Please, please, please,' he silently begged his mother's god but as usual, God's face was turned away and the assistant shook his head and asked, 'Shall I ditch this for you?'

Someone came into the shop behind him.

'All right, Nol?'

Nolly turned, trying to hide his fear but it was only Betfred, a regular at the Saracen and one of Nolly's best customers. Even at this hour of the morning, Fred was immaculately turned out, freshly shaven and dressed in clean jeans and blinding white tee shirt. His jeans actually had creases pressed into them which almost made Nolly smile but he was still really cool for an old bloke, must be fifty or more. Gold glinted at his neck and a gold hoop gleamed from his left ear. Nolly knew there was a Rolex hiding under the sleeve of his leather jacket. Fred never appeared without it.

'All right,' Nolly said, looking down at the scuffed toes of his trainers.

'Usual Fred?' The newsagent handed over a folded newspaper with a smile.

'Respect,' Nolly thought. 'That's what money brings.'

'Give me twenty Silk Cut, as well.'

Nolly noticed the thick gold band on the third finger of his left hand as he handed the money over.

'What's up kid?' Fred said, pocketing his change. 'You look like you seen a ghost. Come next door and have a cup of tea. I'll treat you to a bacon sarnie.'

The long walk from Plotlands had left Nolly tired and hungry. He let Fred lead him into Linda's Butty Bar where the smell of frying bacon made his belly rumble.

'What you doing out so early in the morning anyway?' Fred asked once they were seated.

Nolly sipped his tea. The hot liquid and the heat of the room lowered his defences. Before he knew it he was telling Fred the whole story and it felt good just to let it out. He didn't think Fred was really listening anyway; he was too busy ticking off possibilities in the racing pages of his paper. The bacon butties arrived and Nolly started to wolf his down.

Suddenly Fred looked up and said, 'How much you got then?'

Nolly stopped chewing and hope dawned in his mind. Was Fred going to lend – even give him the money? Everyone said he was super-rich and everyone knew he had a soft spot for young lads, even though he nearly always had a glamorous girl on his arm when he came in the pub. Even as he thought this, his mind recoiled with the thought of what he might have to do in return. He saw his mother shaking her finger at him and mouthing about the sins of Sodom and Gomorrah.

'£70,' he said.

'That won't get you far.' Fred laughed, dropped his bookie's pen and bit into his sandwich. 'Better give it to me.'

'You what?'

'There's a couple of good horses running this afternoon. I'll see what I can do for you.'

Nolly was silent. £70 wasn't much but it was £70 he couldn't afford to lose. Fred seemed okay but how was he to tell really? He might just go off with the lot or at best lose it all on some knackered nag.

Fred seemed to know what he was thinking. 'Look kid, where d'you think all this came from?' He pulled back his sleeve, flashed the Rolex.

It was true Fred had a reputation for picking winners. Nolly hesitated.

'Tell you what. Give me fifty quid. You keep the twenty in case things don't work out, then you still got enough to get you back where you come from.' He sat back and tried to catch Nolly's eye. 'You don't get nowhere in life if you don't take a gamble now and then.'

What did he have to lose? Nolly sighed, pulled the notes out of his pocket, handed over two twenties and a ten.

Fred grinned, got up and hitched his jeans, shoving the rolled up paper in his jacket pocket. 'Meet me back here at three o'clock,' he gripped Nolly's shoulder, 'and don't worry, kid.'

Nolly did worry. He roamed the main street of the town, half frozen with terror as well as cold. He wandered round the single amusement arcade but he was frightened of seeing anyone who knew Tombo and might tell, even though, as yet, there was nothing to tell. The arcade manager looked suspiciously at him, aware that he wasn't spending any money so he ended up in the public library, where at least it was warm, pretending to read a magazine. The library assistant wore a long droopy skirt and shapeless jumper, reminding him of his mother and he wondered how she was, if her medication was working and if she would be pleased to see him if he ever went home.

At last the time came and he went toward the café with leaden feet. His heart felt like it was squeezing into his throat and he struggled for breath. He saw Fred through the window before he even opened the door but it was impossible to tell what he was thinking as he was poring over some betting slips.

'Sorry kid,' he said as soon as Nolly came up, 'didn't do as well as expected.'

It was the end of everything. Nolly sank down in the chair opposite, his mind empty, nothing to say.

'Want a cuppa?' Fred said, reaching into his jacket pocket. Nolly shook his head.

Fred pulled out a wad of notes, began counting out twenties on the table. Nolly's mouth dropped open.

'There you go, kid, £840, best I could do.'

Nolly looked at the money. Something hot and fizzy began spreading inside him. 'What the fuck?' he said.

Fred grinned. 'Now…' He began to take back the notes, counting out £500. 'That's for your debt.'

'But it's £800,' Nolly said.

'£500 will do. You let me take care of Tombo. You take the rest; it'll give you a bit of a start.'

Nolly looked at the money in Fred's hand, the money on the table. The thick gold wedding ring gleamed among the flimsy notes.

'Why are you doing this?' He lifted his eyes to Fred's face.

'I never had a son,' Fred said, 'always wanted a lad of my own. Chrissie and me never had kids and then she upped and left me anyway.' He shrugged. 'Take my advice kid and get out of here. This place is no good for you. Go home to your family. You have got family?'

'My mum,' Nolly said, wondering if he really counted his grandparents as family.

'You go back to your mum, kid. I wish mine was still around. Go on now, clear off.'

Nolly got up, gathered up the notes. 'Thanks Fred,' he said but Fred just whisked a hand at him as if he were an annoying insect. His head stayed down, already engrossed in the sports pages of the evening paper.

Nolly went along the High Street, the £340 burning close to his chest. He would take Fred's advice, leave this dump. As he walked he thought about what to spend the money on. The cash stretched like elastic to cover all the things he wanted; an iPhone, or an iPad, new clothes, driving lessons until more realistic thoughts set in. Nevertheless he deserved a small treat.

He went into the Lord Admiral restaurant, a place where no-one he knew was likely to spot him and wonder how he could afford it and ordered steak and chips. Over the meal, he kept congratulating himself on his good fortune. He could still hardly believe that Fred had helped him without expecting any payback. He wondered how Fred would square things with Tombo who wasn't one to let anyone off with anything. Maybe he owed Fred a favour of some kind. And anyway money talks, Fred exuded a confidence Nolly felt he would never have; without appearing threatening, he seemed to be stronger than Tombo and his henchmen.

He was so busy with it all that he barely tasted his meal, surprised to find his plate empty except for the heap of green peas he'd left on the side. He went out again to find a cold sun shining, brightening the town. Now that his stomach was full and there was money in his pocket the local scene didn't seem so bad. Maybe he wouldn't have to get out of town after all, especially if things were squared with Tombo. He'd got used to it, knew the people here, knew the score. Maybe if he just lay low for a bit, things would go back to normal.

He decided to walk back to his nan's but as he left the main town and passed the Mermaid Inn, a black Merc he knew only too well shot out of the car park and skidded to a stop beside him.

On this occasion Nolly's wish to sit in Tombo's car was granted. He was squashed in the centre of the back seat between the two heavies, one of whom gripped him by the throat while the other pressed a very sharp blade just under his ear.

'I heard you had a bit of a problem,' Tombo's voice was barely audible.

'Don't know what you mean,' Nolly squeaked.

'I heard you ain't got my money.'

'Lies.' Nolly muttered. 'I'll have it by Friday, like you said.' The knife pricked at his throat.

'You better,' Tombo said. Nolly saw him smiling at him in the driving mirror.

Suddenly the pressure was gone, fresh air flooded into the car and Nolly was pushed out onto the pavement, tearing his jeans and grazing both knees. The car sped off, leaving him to walk the two miles back and reflect on his situation. It was dark when he arrived home and his nan and granddad were finishing up their tea.

His nan got his cremated meal out of the oven. 'What have you done to yourself?' she said, looking at his torn jeans.

'Fell over,' Nolly grunted.

'You shouldn't drink,' she sniffed at him before he could say he'd only had a Coke. 'You sound like you're losing your voice, are you coming down with a cold?'

Nolly nodded.

'Best off to bed then after you've eaten.' She peered under his hood. 'You do look a bit peaky.'

By the next morning he'd made his choice. He waited till his nan and granddad left on their weekly shopping trip to the big Morrisons in Rhyl. He replaced the £20 and the £50 he'd 'borrowed' which no one had yet noticed was missing. He took a last look around the old-fashioned living room with its crocheted blankets and heavy furniture before going into the kitchen. He left his key next to the big brown teapot standing on the table. He was about to close the front door when he turned back, looked behind the mantelpiece for an empty envelope, counted out five £20 notes and tucked them inside it. His nan kept a biro behind the clock for doing her wordsearches. Nolly wrote carefully on the back of the envelope in his best school handwriting – *Going home, this is for you for looking after me.* On the front he wrote NAN and put the envelope behind the clock. He didn't want his granddad finding it first.

He went out of the house and began the walk to the bus stop, thinking that he had £240 in his pocket, all his own. He would give his mum £140 when he got home. He would still have £100, which would buy him a new phone.

The bus swept him up and away to Prestatyn where he would catch the train for the first leg of his journey to Telford. He didn't notice Plotlands sliding away into the dark as he stared out of the window. He smiled, thinking how his mother's face would light up when he gave her the money.

Convent Girl

'Tis a terrible thing to find out.' Bridie Dolan looked at the nun across the desk. 'You could have knocked me down with a feather duster when I got the phone call.'

'It was quite a surprise to us too,' Sister Catherine smiled gently. 'All these years, Nuncy's never had a single visitor.'

As if that was my fault, Bridie thought, putting a polite smile on her face. And Nuncy, what kind of a name was that? Sounded like 'dunce.' The woman was probably simple, that's why she'd been put there in the first place. 'Social Services said her name was Agnes, Agnes Doherty.' She tried not to let her thoughts show in her voice.

'Yes of course, her birth name, but when they came in here they were always given new names. I suppose it was to symbolise their new lives here with us, lives gifted to God. Agnes was given the name Annunciata, Nuncy for short. She's always been Nuncy to us.'

'But she wasn't a nun.' Bridie was aghast. The cheek of it, taking your name away, which at the end of the day, if you had nothing else, was your own.

Sister Catherine smiled. Bridie saw the pale light of God in her winter blue eyes and quelled her own anger.

'I know what you're thinking,' the nun said. 'Maybe we need to apologise for things that were done in the past that we wouldn't do today but we learn, we learn, that is the consolation.'

155

Bridie stared. It was hardly consolation to Nuncy or Agnes or whatever her name was or to all the others like her who'd had no one to stand up for them.

'Anyway,' the tranquil eyes weighed her up, 'Social Services are very efficient. They have access to records that we don't. That's how they traced you. The convent is closing; the sisters are going to be split up among other convents. But the ladies – like Nuncy – only a few will be able to live independently. If we can't find relations to take them in, they'll have to go into residential care.' She glanced away out of the window. 'It will be hard for us all; some of us have been here as long as the ladies.'

Well, tough shit for you, Bridie thought but then checked herself, after all these were God's handmaidens. 'Why was she put here in the first place?' she asked. It was a question Social Services had been unable to answer.

If the question made her feel uncomfortable, Sister Catherine didn't show it. Long practice had enabled her to sit immobile and unreacting for hours.

'We don't know. She only came to us in 1980.'

Only! thought Bridie. Thirty-four years– Christ! She looked guiltily at the nun in case she'd sensed her blasphemy.

'People were moved about. We know she came to us from Rockbank, a Liverpool convent but that's long closed and the records are missing. It's likely she came into the system from Ireland as a young girl in the 1950s or 60s, probably because she was pregnant. We do have a birth certificate for 1936, registered in county Clare but that's all.'

'What about the baby?'

The sister shrugged. 'We've no records that there actually was one.'

'But there may be family over in Ireland?' Bridie said hopefully.

'No one's been traced, only her brother – your father.'

'And he's long dead,' Bridie said.

'So we were so pleased when you agreed to come. It's up to you now. If you don't take her we'll find her a place in a local care home.'

She didn't say, 'It's your Catholic duty,' but it was there in her level gaze.

Bridie looked down in her lap. It was years since she'd been to confession or even to church but in her heart she believed and it was for them all, wasn't it? That's what catholic meant – for everybody. She thought of her own five kids; as if she'd ever let them go into care but things were different then. She knew how attitudes had been even when she was a girl, visiting her mother's relations in Wexford.

Michael would go mad. She'd have to phone him. He wouldn't be home till the end of the month, when the tarmacking contract would end and he'd leave his brothers in Liverpool and come back to the family.

'Can I see her?' she asked, her mind almost made up.

Sister Catherine smiled her sweet smile. 'I wouldn't want to get her hopes up unnecessarily. She'd be terribly upset if – I know it's a big commitment and I know it depends on personalities but even if you could give me some idea of your thoughts, if you think you might…'

'If we get on all right,' Bridie said, feeling as if she was stepping into a great hole.

Sister Catherine got to her feet. Bridie was surprised to see she wore a short navy pinafore dress that showed her legs. 'Come along then, I'll have her brought to a private room for you and someone will bring you some tea.'

She didn't look like an Agnes. Bridie had imagined someone serene and dignified with curled silver hair as she followed Sister Catherine through a labyrinth of corridors. When the nun finally threw open a door, Bridie was lost for words.

The room was too small to contain anyone else so this had to be her. The woman was tiny, perched on the edge of a hard chair in front of a small table. Her body was as stick thin and dried looking as the furniture. She shrank back as Bridie and the nun entered.

'Sit up properly, Nuncy,' Sister Catherine commanded and the poor little thing jerked to attention. 'This is your niece, Mrs Dolan.'

'Bridie,' Bridie interrupted.

The woman's eyes swivelled to her and back to Sister Catherine.

'You remember, I told you she was coming to see you.' She smiled at Nuncy, showing small pointed teeth. Bridie thought there was something predatory about Sister Catherine's smiles.

'Sister Martha will be along in a minute with tea. I'll leave you to get to know each other.' She swished out and the door closed behind her.

The room seemed even smaller. Bridie stared at Agnes. Agnes stared back.

'Agnes…' Bridie began but the woman seemed to shrivel in front of her, wrapping her arms round herself. Her chair scraped backwards.

'Nuncy,' she whispered, her pale lips barely moving.

'That's not your name though, is it?' Bridie's voice seemed to bounce at high volume off the walls of the little room but she was determined to start as she meant

158

to go on. She took in the dull stare, the quivering rat-sharp features; the lank grey hair that was parted and gripped back like a 1950s school child. Her eyes travelled over the other's flat chest, the colourless greyish crimplene pinafore dress. It was hard to think of anyone ever making her pregnant. Hot pity rushed through her body, churning her belly and driving a flush to her cheeks. 'It's Agnes,' she said, 'your real name is Agnes. Do you remember Ireland and my father – your brother Declan?'

Agnes's face changed. It was the eyes, Bridie thought, trying not to stare. The dullness was gone and bright and black they fixed on Bridie's face. There was a dark spark in them that spoke to Bridie, although she didn't know what it said, but she felt lighter, encouraged. Not an idiot, then.

Agnes's lip drew back to show rodent teeth and her mouth opened as if she was going to speak but the moment shattered as an obese nun barged into the room bearing a tea tray.

Bridie sighed and let the net curtain fall, veiling the sight of the skinny figure battling against the wind that blew across the dunes. At first she'd been too afraid to let Agnes out on her own but the Plotlands beach or the sea, Bridie wasn't sure which, seemed to be a magnet for her.

After the first few days when Bridie didn't have time to keep walking with her (after all she had her own five kids to try to keep an eye on without the extra burden of a dotty old lady) she'd explained to Agnes that she mustn't go out alone because of the dangers of the shivering sands where that bloke had sunk and died a couple of years previously.

There was also the traffic, although there wasn't much traffic in the early spring but surely Agnes wasn't used to traffic and couldn't be trusted to negotiate the Plotlands road safely. Throughout this lecture, Agnes said nothing but stared with her hard little black eyes and then promptly slipped out the minute Bridie had gone upstairs to make the beds. Bridie looked out of Maire's window and saw her, bent as the marram grass, heading along the top path, silhouetted against the blustering clouds.

She had to send Brian, her eldest, out to bring her back and she thought that maybe she could get the kids to take turns to play chaperone but Brian made up a song about her that went, 'Nuncy duncy, deaf and dumb, wanks in bed and sucks her thumb', which he taught, not only to his brothers and sisters but to all the local kids, so that didn't work out so well. It was true that Agnes sucked her thumb; Bridie had seen her doing it when she'd taken her a morning cup of tea so she guessed the kids had been spying on her. She'd barely spoken since she'd arrived; no wonder the kids thought she was weird. Bridie wondered what on earth she was going to do with her.

On the fourth day, she took her on the bus to Prestatyn and got her registered with the family doctor. Agnes submitted meekly to being checked over and was given a clean bill of health pending transfer of her medical records and blood test results..

'Why won't she talk?' Bridie asked the doctor but he had no answer.

'Give her time,' he advised, 'and maybe ask her social worker.'

Bridie didn't care for social workers, they were mostly interfering young madams, all certificates and no life skills. Look what they'd done to Milly Pink, putting that Sonia in charge of the shop. Bridie missed her chats with Milly who was rarely seen at the counter nowadays. The shop was being transformed into a sort of arty-farty place selling jars of olives and scented candles and boxes of fancy chocolates that no one who lived in Plotlands wanted. It wouldn't last long selling stuff like that and then where would they be, having to walk to the garage on the main road for a drop of milk or a loaf in winter when the holiday camp shop was shut?

Bridie took Agnes into Cantelino's ice cream parlour and bought her a large cone with a chocolate flake on top. When she saw how her face lit up she felt glad and rewarded for taking her in and she persevered with talking to her and asking questions that remained unanswered.

After a week of silence and giving Bridie the slip to roam the wastelands along the shore, Agnes returned one day of her own accord, her hair blown into a bird's nest. She took off her coat, went to the cutlery drawer and took out a kitchen knife. She sat down beside Bridie and began to help her peel the potatoes.

'It's a start,' she told Michael when he phoned her that night. He was more sympathetic than she'd expected him to be. She supposed it was something to do with that veneration of the mother that a lot of Catholic men seemed to have, some sort of confusion put in their minds at an early age by the Church, that they never quite got to grips with; something that transferred the honour due to Mary, mother of the Church to any old woman who possibly had been a mother.

161

It only seemed to apply to old women though, Bridie thought as Michael waffled down the phone about how he was glad to accept responsibility for the auld duck. It hadn't stopped him blacking her own eye once or twice when he'd been too free with the whisky and she'd been too free with her tongue. She'd put a stop to that by taking her mother's advice and cracking him over the head with a cast-iron griddle, a prudent but until then unused wedding gift from her Aunty Bernie on her mother's side. After this he'd kept his fists to himself.

She said goodnight to Michael and put the phone down. She could hear Maire and Catherine fighting in their room. Maire was always giving out lately because Cathy's room had been given up so Agnes could have it and Maire was forced to share with Cathy. Bridie peeped through the half-open lounge door. Agnes was sitting entranced in front of the TV. At least it kept her in one place, Bridie thought as she climbed the stairs to the source of increasingly bloodcurdling screams.

'What's all this?' She burst into the pandemonium of the room. Cathy, purple-faced, jumped and screamed on her bed. Maire screamed back from her own bed on the opposite side of the room. A piece of string had been laid across the carpet, dividing the room in two. On Maire's side, clothes and make up were flung everywhere. On Cathy's side, dolls, teddies and books lay in disordered heaps.

'She won't let me out,' Cathy roared, tears almost squirting from her eyes. 'Mammy, tell her to let me out!'

'She's not standing on my side of the floor,' Maire screamed. 'She spilt paint all over my new frock, Mammy.'

'Shut up and stop being a pair of eejits,' Bridie shouted loud enough to drown them both out. 'Do you want me to have to tell your da? Then there'll be no present for either of yous when he comes home.'

Both girls were silent for a moment and before they could start up again Bridie shouted, 'Now pick up all this mess and Cathy, you get into your jammies now and don't let me hear no more. What must your Aunty Agnes think of you?'

They stared sullenly at her and made no reply. Bridie went down the stairs counting. She got to eight before the racket started up again. And this was before the lads got home and started playing their heavy metal or grunge or whatever it was called.

Agnes was still sitting in front of the telly, her eyes following the screen as if she were somehow electronically connected to it. Bridie looked at her childish little legs, her almost white tights, her dark red plush slippers, her feet neatly lined up together. Her pink scalp shone through the merciless part in her hair. Bridie tried to imagine her as a wild Irish rose, innocent but falling, falling for some handsome soldier or maybe a blacksmith's lad. She'd recently seen a film where just such a young girl with long, black hair that blew in the wind, had been courted and abandoned by a blacksmith lad so handsome that any woman would have given in to him. She looked doubtfully at Agnes.

'Are you enjoying the programme, Aunty?'

Agnes seemed to have a penchant for soaps. Bridie didn't follow them herself, mostly being too busy round the house to watch much TV but she realised the storyline Agnes was watching involved an unwanted pregnancy as a result of one of the characters having a fling with a married neighbour. Her first urge was to switch off the telly but then she reasoned she had no idea how much sense Agnes made of the programmes she watched so avidly.

Still, she switched channels saying, 'There's a nice programme about dogs on the other side. Shall I make us a cup of tea?' Agnes didn't reply but turned her head slowly to look at Bridie and her eyes were liquorice black, shiny with tears.

That night, when the house was at last quiet, Bridie went to her own bed. Usually she was glad of the peace and the chance to be alone but that night the big bed seemed cold and the room full of shadows. The wind came whistling in from the sea, skirling round the gutters to whisper at the window frames that there were secrets in the house.

Now Bridie was tormented all the time, not so much by these secrets, hidden away in Agnes's head, but by the whereabouts of the products of them, so to speak. If Agnes had borne a child, what had become of him or her? Her few forays into questions about Agnes's past were met with the usual wall of silence and there were no more tears.

The social worker, when she finally arrived, was of little help either. Her name was Maisie and she spent half an hour closeted with Agnes in her room and then joined Bridie for a cup of tea to tell her everything seemed satisfactory.

'It's a pleasure to see things working so well,' she said, rustling her papers. She looked hopefully at Bridie.

'Oh to be sure,' Bridie said, thankful that it was a school day so there was no mayhem going on in the house. 'It's just…'

Maisie looked up, contracting her brows at the doubtful note in Bridie's voice.

'…I can't help wondering what happened to the child.'

'Child?'

'The sister at the convent said she probably had a child, an unwanted child.' There was something terribly sad in that adjective. Bridie bit her lips as the sound of it escaped them.

Maisie frowned, flicked through her papers. 'There's no mention of a child here. Has she said anything to you?'

'No,' Bridie said, 'it's just a feeling.' She thought of the tears and the way Agnes sometimes stared at Polly, Bridie's youngest, till poor Polly would run and hide behind Bridie in terror of the scary old lady.

Maisie sighed and leaned across the table, looking earnest. 'We come across a lot of women like this you know, women with no proper record to tell us what's happened to them. Sometimes they make things up, invent children they never had, things that never happened. It's a better story than facing the fact that their family gave them away.'

'Gave them away?' Bridie gawped.

'Sometimes they couldn't afford to feed them, or they might have been a bit…' she searched for the politically correct term. 'They might have had some kind of learning difficulty, might have been too much of a burden on the family.'

'Oh.' Bridie thought about it; it would account for Agnes's reluctance to speak.

'The main thing now is to concentrate on the present,' Maisie said, brightening. 'Make the most of what life she has left. It might help to take her to church. She tells me she hasn't been?'

'She spoke to you?' Bridie felt indignant. Why would Agnes speak to this stranger when she wouldn't open her mouth at home?

'Well, not exactly.' Maisie tinkled a little laugh. 'Just nods and shakes of the head. Confession might be the thing to loosen her tongue?' Maisie was employed by Catholic Social Services. She tried not to look disapproving when Bridie faltered that it was a long time since she had been herself.

The thought of the length of time it would take her to confess her sins weighed Bridie down for the rest of the day but she felt that perhaps Maisie was right. The priest might succeed in getting Agnes to talk where they had both failed and she could hardly take her to Mass without going to confession herself now could she?

She was unprepared for Agnes's reaction when she suggested a visit to St Thomas the Apostle the next day for morning Mass. Agnes's face contorted with horror and she dropped the spoon of rice pudding she was about to put in her mouth. The spoon clattered in the bowl and splattered its contents over Maire's new top. 'After me taking all afternoon to get the paint out of it,' Bridie thought as she interpreted Agnes's body language.

Maire jumped up from the table, making piggish squeals but everyone ignored her, fascinated by the thin, horrified wail that was coming from Agnes's mouth. Before any of them could react, she shot to her feet and ran out of the kitchen. They all looked at each other, astonished as they listened to the sound of her feet thudding up the stairs. She had always been so silent.

When Bridie went upstairs to her she found the door bolted from the inside and all her pleas for it to be unfastened were ignored. She tried cajoling, with no success, then grew angry and demanding, rattling the door fruitlessly.

'You come out now, Agnes and stop playing up like a spoilt child now.'

Silence.

Eventually Bridie gave up.

'Well, if she wants to lock herself in up there it's her loss,' she told Michael when there was still no sign of her at 8 o'clock, despite the lure of the soaps.

The phone line echoed with Michael's laughter. 'I'd be mighty scairt meself to meet the priest now, Bridie, and so would you I reckon. Let her be, if she don't want to go.'

After this, Bridie went upstairs with a hot drink and called through the door in her gentlest voice. 'We won't be going to the church if you don't want to, Aunty, so come on and open the door; I've brought you a nice cup of cocoa.'

But there was still no response.

'I'll leave it here then, so?' Bridie said, setting it down outside the door.

When she went to bed the cup was still there, the cocoa coated with a cold skin and it was still there the next morning and Agnes's place remained empty at the breakfast table. What to do? Bridie worried, she was responsible for her after all. What if she'd taken a stroke or a heart attack or something? But breaking down the door seemed overly dramatic and there'd be hell to pay if Michael came home and found it smashed. Bridie went upstairs and knocked and rattled once more, all five kids listening behind her. She put her ear to the door but all was silent.

'What about the window?' Sean said and they all trooped outside to look and saw that the window was slightly ajar.

'I'll get up.' Brian puffed himself up, acting the alpha male of the family in his daddy's absence.

'He's too big, let me.' Sean danced with excitement.

Bridie looked at the silver birch that stood close to the house and pursed her lips. 'He's right,' she told Brian. 'Up you go then, but mind you don't frighten her now.'

Sean monkeyed up the tree like lightning, watched by Sally Thornton from the house opposite. Bridie wanted to tell her to go in and mind her own business. After all, she'd no reason to point the finger with that paedophile husband of hers. Bridie'd been terrified for her own kids once it came out what he'd done. Thankfully he'd been put away but she'd be glad when someone bought the Thornton's house and Sally Thornton moved away, so there'd be no chance of him coming back. No sign of any buyers yet though so she still had to live with her after all and their relationship was already often strained with her complaining about Brian's music and Sean's erratic football. There was a sudden squawking like a disturbed hencoop as Brian's rear end and flailing legs disappeared through the window.

'Mother of God, he's fallen on top of her,' Bridie fisted her hand in her mouth as she ran into the house but the bedroom door was open and Agnes was standing on the landing in her dressing gown and slippers.

Bridie waited till the kids had all gone to school and Agnes had devoured two boiled eggs and four slices of toast. 'So, you don't want to go to Mass, you don't have to,' she said. 'There's no need to lock yourself in your room and cause all that kerfuffle.'

Agnes regarded her over her mug of tea.

'Did you not go when you were in the convent?' Bridie tried.

Agnes's face took on a mutinous expression and she shook her head.

'It's a long time since I've been,' Bridie said. 'It's hard to go to confession after a long time. Is that how it is?' She poured herself another mug of tea as if she wasn't at all concerned.

Agnes put down her mug and made a pushing motion with both hands as if to shoo Bridie away.

'How long is it?'

Silence but Agnes's anguished stare was needle sharp.

'All the time you were there, in the convent?'

This time, almost a nod, her eyes never wavered.

'Why?' Bridie said softly. 'You had a child, was that it? Was that why they sent you away – your family?'

There was movement but it was only Agnes's hands, writhing in her lap.

'A child is never a sin,' Bridie said. 'Did the father abandon you then?'

Agnes's eyes lost their fixity. They moved and darkened, rolling away from Bridie and the present to something, somewhere else, as if she was looking back, back into her history. She lifted her hands, made that pushing motion again. Whispery sounds came out of her mouth. Bridie bent her head closer to listen.

'Pushed him,' the words hissed out.

'Pushed who?'

'Fergus s s s, off the t t t-ractor. It was s-s-spring, it was hot, the s-s-sun on my face. He was laughing.' Her voice grew stronger, the words followed each other

169

hissing and swirling as if she was talking to herself. 'I went to as-s-sk him, about the wedding. I was four months gone, hadn't even told my mam for fear of my da.'

Bridie held her breath but Agnes didn't seem to be aware of her.

'He laughed. I was looking up at him. The sun was behind his head like the pictures of the saints and he laughed and said he wasn't ready to marry. I climbed up on the footrest to plead with him but there was no moving him and then I lost my temper. Mammy always said I let my mouth run away with me.' She stopped, a hand to her mouth, her eyes returning.

'It's all right,' said Bridie.

'I pushed him and he fell and the tractor went right over him before I could stop it.'

There was silence for a moment and Bridie saw a tear seep under Agnes's eyelid.

'I ran away, ran away and left him. I didn't tell no one. When the men went back after their dinner they found him dead.'

'You didn't tell it was you?'

'No one ever knew.' She looked up and her eyes were black and bright once more, her hands still now in her lap.

'And the child?'

'The nuns took him.' Her face clouded for a moment then cleared. 'It was for the best.'

'So, I've a murderer under my roof,' Bridie thought as she lay in bed that night. Michael was due home the next day but already she knew she wouldn't tell him, wouldn't tell anyone, any more than she'd tell about

170

that first child of her own. Pretty much the same story only in her case it had been the lad with the Italian motorbike who'd come to live in the village and had struck her head so full of stars that she stopped hearing her mother's warnings and then it was too late.

But she'd been the lucky one. God had answered her as she'd prayed like Our Lord to be relieved of the burden. And after seven or eight weeks there'd been barely anything to show for all that worry and fear, but even so, there'd always been that sadness and those questions lingering in her mind whenever she let it roll back to the past.

History was full of if onlys and what might have beens and some things maybe were best not spoken of. Maybe someday Agnes might want to find out about her child but that was up to her. Bridie resolved that her own lips should be sealed on the subject.

The next day Agnes began to talk.

Smoke Without Fire

Fred relaxed once he turned onto the M56. It had been a good day at the races. Haydock was one of his favourite courses and the Belfair Chase was always a red letter day, being the last race of the season. It helped that it was handy for North Wales too. Odds were he'd be back in time for a few pints at his local before the evening started properly.

It was good to unwind after a big win: after the excitement of the turf, going home with a good wodge in his inside pocket and the Jag purring along, eating up the motorway as if it knew the way home. Hot Chocolate's *You Sexy Thing* came on the radio and he sang along with Errol Brown, thinking it would have been nice if Gemma had come along. Winning always made him feel horny and the song lyrics brought it on but it was a sleepy kind of sexual feeling. He only realised he was losing concentration when an artic honked at him and he saw he was straying into the next lane. He pulled back and turned the radio off.

The Chester services sign loomed up and he indicated and turned off. Passing the Days Inn motel he thought about Gemma again. They could have made a night of it, if she hadn't started that stupid row: booked in here or even somewhere in Liverpool. That would have been better; they could have got a good meal and gone to the casinos. But Gemma was blowing hot and cold lately. He sensed that soon she would go for good. They all did, once the novelty of the money wore off

173

and they realised that no matter how well he treated them, there wasn't going to be a wedding ring. Marriage was a non-runner. Look what had happened with Chrissie. He was still reeling from the aftershock of the divorce. He wasn't going to let himself in for that again. Anyway, since yesterday, Gemma wouldn't answer his calls and she was ignoring his texts. It was going to cost him to win her round but was it worth it?

The service station sparkled like a pleasure palace against the backdrop of the night and Fred went willingly into its maw, glad to be swallowed up in the warmth and the smell of coffee and fast food. He fancied a burger but needed to watch his waistline; Gemma'd been commenting lately on his love handles. It was another indication that the relationship was foundering. He'd begun to notice she was always finding fault with him these days.

He settled for a large cappuccino and fished in his pocket for the race card he'd kept to check the form against the horses' actual performances. Bellinger's Boy had done him proud today and he'd have to look out for him in next year's steeplechases. There was the state of the ground and the seasonal weather to calculate though. He knew that Bellinger's Boy favoured wintry conditions and wet ground. What he pulled out of his pocket though was the letter that the postman had brought just as he was getting in the Jag. He glanced at it, saw Chrissie's writing on the envelope and his good mood evaporated.

Another begging letter for more money - as if he really owed her anything. He'd let her have a good divorce settlement but she was always asking for money for something. It wasn't as if they'd had kids. That was probably half the problem. Of course, everything was made out to be his fault; his playing away from home had been the main accusation in the divorce papers. It had been easier to let it go at that than keep fighting, but really some of the responsibility had been hers. If she'd taken an interest, joined in his lifestyle, he wouldn't have been so tempted to stray. Racing meets, casinos, there was always plenty of eye-candy and if it went further, well, what man would refuse when it was offered on a plate, especially when he was getting nothing at home any more?

He shoved the unopened letter back in his pocket, too tense now to concentrate on the race card. Flashing lights across the way from the café area caught his eye and he felt in his pockets for change. Slot machines were for suckers, a real bad bet, but it just might take his mind off Chrissie. Surely she'd known that deep down he'd always loved her, still did? He counted out five pound coins, no more, money he was happy to waste. There were four machines, a couple of racing games and a couple of bandits and a kid was playing one of them. He looked no more than fifteen but there was no one round to shoo him off. Fred put his first pound in, won two back. He wasn't really concentrating. He was thinking about Chrissie, how she'd fleeced him after twenty-six years of marriage, was still fleecing him. Had it really only been about money? It hurt, it really hurt still, even six months after the final papers had come.

He thought of the empty flat waiting for him and put another pound in the slot. The flat wasn't a home, just a stopgap, impersonal. The sooner he got a proper place the better. There were two new property developments he was considering, both built by the same developer. One was in Meliden, very upmarket, not far from the Falls resort spa, the other at Plotlands, right on the coast. At the moment he had to be careful with his cash and he wasn't used to that. The divorce had hit him hard in the pocket and it would take time to recover. Besides, Plotlands had nostalgia value for him. It existed in a timewarp of the sixties and seventies, he still went there now and then to play the ancient slot machines in the decrepit arcade, reliving childhood days out. He even liked the name of the Plotlands development, *Badger's End*, it sounded kind of countrified. He realised he was down to his last pound, fed it into the machine and was rewarded with a shower of coins rattling into the tray. The kid looked over at him.

Fred looked at the soft curve of his cheek, the suggestion of a downy beard contrasting with the child's eyes looking enviously at the heap of money Fred scooped from the tray.

'Here,' Fred said, holding out the money, 'Have a game on me.'

The kid looked frightened, suspicion flooding his eyes.

'Go on,' Fred said, 'take it. Never look a gift horse in the mouth.'

The kid looked round as if for advice. He stared into the crowd of people eating in the café area, presumably reassuring himself that his parents were nearby. 'Okay, thanks,' He took the money and moved over to a car racing game, fed in a coin and he was away.

He was good, Fred thought, watching him manoeuvre but the next moment the kid lost concentration and crashed.

'You like cars?' Fred twirled on his seat.

The boy nodded.

'Old enough to drive yet?' Fred asked although he could tell the kid was a couple of years shy.

'Not yet,' the boy shook his head.

176

'What car would you have, if you had plenty of money, could buy whatever you wanted?'

The kid shrugged. 'I dunno, a Porsche maybe?'

Small dreams, Fred thought, if it was me, I'd be thinking Maserati, but then a kid's world is small. He thought back to himself as a teenager, his thoughts set no higher than a Citroen Dyane. He'd been the only child of a single mother and they'd been piss poor.

'I used to have a Porsche,' he told the kid, 'but now I like a bit of comfort, something smooth.' The kid was jingling the money in his pocket, anxious to get back to the game. Fred thought of the keyring with the model Porsche on it that Chrissie had given him one Christmas. He remembered it was still in the glove compartment of the Jag where he'd shoved it when he got the new car. Maybe the kid would like it. He'd got no use for it and he was a nice kid.

'I got something in the car you might like,' he told the boy. 'I'll go and get it.'

The Jag was waiting out in the night, best car in the car park.

'This yours?' a voice said and Fred turned to see the kid had followed him out. He was looking at the car as if he'd like to stroke it but didn't dare.

'She's my best girl,' Fred said and opened the door.

They came from nowhere, a blur of black jumpers and trousers and a clatter of heavy feet. Fred was seized from behind, jerked round. 'What????' he managed to get out as he glimpsed their security badges and saw the fat, red-faced woman struggling to run up to them. Through the rushing of his blood Fred heard her wail of anguish, like a cow calling for a lost calf. She got hold of the kid and shook him.

'What have I told you, what have I told you?' she shouted over and over, then she folded him in her arms

177

as he started to cry. 'Dirty bastard!' she shouted at Fred and he realised that everyone walking in the car park had stopped to watch and lifting his gaze to the service station he saw the pale blobs of gawping faces at the café tables.

'I haven't done…' he started but the two heavies cut him off. One took the key from his hand and locked the door.

'Come on you,' the other said. They took an arm each and jostled him inside and through a door marked PRIVATE into a little bare cupboard of a room with just a desk and a couple of chairs. 'Wait here,' they said, as if he had any choice, and then they left. He heard the door lock behind them, saw one of them stare at him through the small square glass door panel before they went away.

As soon as they'd gone, Fred pulled out his phone and tried to phone Gemma and then Chrissie but neither answered. There wasn't really anyone else except his bookie and he didn't want everyone to know his business. It wasn't the kind of thing you wanted broadcast. Time passed as Fred considered his position. Of course it was ludicrous; anyone who knew him knew he wouldn't hurt a hair on anyone's head. But it looked bad, he had to admit. He was known for befriending young lads but that was all it was. He didn't like to see any kid in trouble, like Nolly Perkins. He'd felt sorry for the lad, under threat from Tombo Charles for the sake of a couple of hundred quid. It was a fortune to a kid like that, an impossible sum to raise and even though Fred had a bad day at the races, he'd given Nolly the money, let him think he'd won it.

Fred had a hard life when he was a young lad and he knew how these kids felt. Each and every one looked so vulnerable, tenderly dangling between being a child and an adult in a cold, hard world. They all reminded him of himself and more importantly of that son he'd longed for; the boy he would have played football with, taken swimming, gentling him into the ways of the world until he was old enough to share football matches and propping up the bar at Fred's local.

'You don't always get what you want,' he sang under his breath, forgetting where he was at that moment until a noise in the corridor startled him and he jumped up to see a face peering at him through the glass door panel. He went to the door but the face ducked away and the corridor was silent. How long was he to be kept here? Because of the row with Gemma, no one would be expecting him to be anywhere tonight; his absence at the pub wouldn't be noticed because he hadn't been there much while he'd been seeing Gem.

The two heavies hadn't even given him the chance to get angry, protest his innocence and demand his solicitor, although the only solicitor Fred had specialised in divorce and there was a fat chance of getting hold of him on a Saturday evening.

He was going to be arrested for sure but would they keep him in custody? Who would vouch for his innocence or stand his bail? Gemma? Chrissie? He realised he couldn't count on either. Chrissie was full of bitterness and Gemma? – well they'd only been going out a few weeks and last night she'd sounded like she hated him. He thought of his casual pub and racing buddies; there wasn't one he could really call a friend. They would disappear like straw in the wind at the hint of any trouble.

If only the damned kid hadn't followed him out to the car. Why the hell did he do that? Maybe the boy would tell them it was all innocent, friendly stuff but would they believe him? The mother had come at him like a battling Amazon.

There was a fumbling at the door then one of the security guards came in, followed by two police officers bulky in hi-vis jackets. The female officer looked tiny inside her huge coat. Fred noted her flawless skin and pale blonde hair tied up under her hat in a neat plait. She had beautiful brown eyes but the look she turned on him froze his balls. He looked from one to another, saw the same barely veiled disgust and condemnation on the faces of all three and words shrivelled in his mouth.

It was nearly one-thirty in the morning when they let him out of the police station and he'd expected to spend the night in the cells but Gemma had finally come up trumps and bailed him out. He hadn't been charged with anything but his head was rattling from the vicious verbal attack and their dirty suggestions. They'd made it clear that in their minds he was guilty and there would almost certainly be further questioning depending on what the kid and his mother said when they were interviewed later in the day.

Fred stood on the steps of the police station while Gemma rummaged in her bag for her car keys. The lights of a casino gleamed further down the street but he was too tired to be drawn by its lure. He thought of the bonhomie of his usual Saturday night, knocking back Scotch and playing the tables in the soporific perfumed warmth that surrounded the female croupiers. But right now all he wanted was to get home, run a hot bath and wash out the grime the police had put in his mind and the dirty smells of sweat and stale coffee that had soaked into his pores in the grubby interview room.

'This is the last thing I do for you,' Gemma snapped as they got in her car. She rammed the key in the ignition and he looked across at her, surprised by the flinty set of her jaw and the way she looked straight at the windscreen, refusing to turn to him. 'This is it. It's over.' She gunned the accelerator and the car shot out of the parking space.

'You don't think…?' Fred felt as if she'd punched him.

'I don't know what to think,' she hissed through clenched teeth as she drove back towards the motorway. 'How do I know?'

Fred couldn't think of anything to say. Gemma seemed to have a cold shield around her that made him shrink and froze his thoughts. The more he looked at her in the dimly lit car, the more she resembled an alien. How could he ever have fancied such a creature? The car was a bubble of silence, Fred as eager to get out as she was to be rid of him. At last the Chester services sign came up and she pulled in and stopped in the car park.

As he started to get out, she seemed to soften. 'Look, do you want to get a coffee?' She leaned sideways, turning towards him, her face chiselled from shadows. He couldn't tell what she was thinking. He looked at the swell of her breasts rising out of her tight top, a smudge of shadow defining the cleft between them.

'It's okay Gem,' he said, 'forget it.' He walked off to look for the Jag.

The drive home did something to soothe his nerves. The night was dark and velvet with little traffic about. The tightness in his head began to ease and as he drove into Prestatyn he was thinking about a good stiff single

181

malt. The casino lights still glimmered and he saw Lenny, the doorman, standing outside. Suddenly he felt the need for human company. He parked the car and went over.

'You're late tonight Fred.' Lenny's welcoming smile cheered him.

'You don't know the half of it,' Fred said.

'I'm on my break in a minute. Come in, I'll buy you a drink.'

Fred woke about noon, cracking his eyes open to bright sunlight as he'd forgotten to draw the bedroom curtains. He looked out of the window and saw the Jag was not in its parking space then he remembered he had left it outside the casino and got a taxi home.

'Oh shit!' He lay back in bed. What had he done? What had he SAID? Had he told Lenny all that had happened the night before? He couldn't remember. It was easier to slide back into sleep and forget the whole shitty mess.

When he woke again towards evening, he was in a different frame of mind. His head was clear and after a shower, some hot coffee and a bacon sandwich he was ready to go. He had to get to Lenny and make sure he didn't spill his guts to everyone in the club.

The Jag was just as he had left it except for a fresh smattering of seagull droppings but Lenny wasn't on the door, there was a new bloke Fred had never seen before.

'Jimmy,' the new bloke said in answer to Fred's question. 'It's Lenny's night off.'

Fred went inside. He thought he saw Lenny at the bar but when the man turned to speak to the barman, he realised it was someone else. The barman whispered something and the man turned to stare at Fred then looked away.

'Usual please, George,' Fred said jauntily, although something was making him feel uncomfortable. George didn't meet his eyes but turned his back and began pouring Fred's favourite whisky. Fred turned uneasily, surveyed the gaming room. No one was looking at him but there was something deliberate in that. Hairs prickled on the back of his neck.

George slid the drink over to him but before he could grasp the glass another hand came from behind him and lifted it out of his reach.

'Sorry Fred, can't serve you I'm afraid.'

'What?' Fred whirled to face the club manager, immaculate in bow tie and dinner jacket. 'What are you talking about?'

'I mean you're not welcome here any more. Not after what's happened.'

'What's happened?' Fred spluttered for a second till the penny dropped. 'That bastard Lenny,' he said.

'We don't want any trouble.' The manager fiddled with his shirt cuffs. Fred knew he'd been a handy lad at one time but now he could afford to pay someone else to do the dirty work. He could see the new doorman hovering at the entrance watching for a wrong move from Fred.

'For fuck's sake Frankie, I've been coming here for years. You know I wouldn't do anything like that.'

'We don't know anything, Fred. That's why we have to be careful. We don't want those sort of people in here.'

'But…' Fred said and then stopped. The barman had taken his drink away to the back of the bar and the bloke on the stool was openly staring, waiting for Fred's response.

'I'll have to ask you to leave, Sir.' Frankie gave a barely perceptible nod to the doorman.

'Sir?' Fred gave a barking laugh. 'I've not been convicted of anything,' he shouted to the room, only then noticing the silence and inactivity at the tables. They were all watching the circus and he was the star performer.

'Come along please Sir.' The doorman came up like a bulky mother penguin intent on ushering him to the door. As he passed the roulette table Fred heard a woman whisper to the croupier, 'There's no smoke without fire.'

Badger's End

Who'd have thought that coming to work in Aunty Milly's grotty old shop would open up an opportunity like this? Sonia locked the door of the shop for the very last time and turned away.

The key went into an envelope in her handbag, ready to be taken to the council offices now that the compulsory purchase was completed. She didn't look back or think about the history of the place as she walked the few yards to her new job. Her mind was full of the shining future, the new buildings that would rise from the ashes of the old dump. She was leaving it all behind, her mother and the endless babysitting for the younger kids and of course she'd got away from no-good Malc as her mother always called him.

She bit her lip at the memory of the black eyes and the broken wrist he'd once given her. She still felt shame, thinking of her mother's expression each time she came home with injuries and each time she went back to him. He was just so persuasive and she'd felt so in love with him, so sure he would change. Well, that was all over. She'd come to her senses once she'd come to Plotlands. Coming to look after Aunty Milly had been a godsend. Her mum had jumped at the idea and she knew she would never tell Malc where she'd gone. But Aunt Milly and the dirty old shop were only stepping stones. Sonia had much better things in mind. She'd turned twenty last year and it was time to make a life for herself.

A gravel path had been laid across the mud of the building site to her office. It was only a portakabin but it held promises of pinnacles and palaces, a bit like the poems Sonia had studied for her English GCSE. Her heels skittered as she picked her way through the grit but they were the only shoes to wear for this kind of job, the only shoes that went well with her navy blue business suit. So what if it would take her a year to pay for the outfit on her mum's catalogue? It had already paid for itself by helping her to get the job and maybe attracting the attention of the area manager, Mike Martland.

'Morning Sonia.' Jim Fawcett was already at his desk, similarly sharp-suited. He was okay but Sonia was setting her sights higher now she was on the ladder to success. It was nearing the end of her second week and already she'd graduated from filing notes and letters to entering data on the computer. It wasn't easy getting used to a different work environment and familiarising herself with the finicky tea and coffee requirements of Jim and Mike. She discovered that, like most men, they liked to be fussed over so she'd secured favour by producing special chocolate biscuits, salvaged from the shop stock, whenever Mike came and making sure she always looked her best.

It wasn't easy either, after a full day at a new job full of anxiety-producing new tasks, having to spend all her spare time clearing out the shop, disposing of the stock and visiting Aunty Milly in the care home. Not to mention dealing with her mum's constant agitated phone calls as she tried to direct operations from a distance. But she'd been determined and now she was reaping the rewards. Next week she would graduate to cold calling and Mike had intimated that once the show house was up, if all went well, a junior would be brought in to handle the filing and she would be trained up in sales. Badger's End was only one of Rosebrier Homes's projects in the region and Mike told her there would be a profitable career for the right girl.

She was going to be that right girl. She stiffened her spine as she sat behind her desk and put on a gleaming smile, all the time she was riffling through her filing tray, imagining herself showing some eager young couple round a beautiful new home. By then, she'd be wearing a real designer suit, Jimmy Choo shoes, not a hair out of place and they'd so want to be like her, to buy the lovely home she was offering.

She'd have a lovely home too. For now she was lodging with Mrs Fairweather and her disgusting cat but once she got into selling, started earning commission, she'd get her own flat: Prestatyn maybe or Rhyl. Maybe she'd even be able to buy one of Rosebrier's homes at a discount price. Then she'd need a car of course…

The ring of her telephone broke into her daydream but she didn't mind. She was at the frontline of the Badger's End enterprise and she loved the sense of power that gave her.

'Good morning, Rosebrier Homes, you're through to the Badger's End Sales office. You're speaking to Sonia. How may I help?'

Of course they didn't want her. It was always Jim or sometimes Mike they asked for but that would change.

On her way home, Sonia saw Bill Wicklow getting off the Flint bus carrying the Evening Leader. 'It's a sorry end, this,' he grumbled.

'What?' Sonia said, unplugging her MP3 player. She was still thinking about the wonderful phone call earlier when Mike had rung offering to take her on some sales calls at another development. To show her the ropes, he'd said.

187

'This,' Bill said, wagging the paper in front of her face. 'I've had to go to the garage for it now the shop's shut. It's a disgrace.'

Sonia shrugged. It wasn't that far to the garage. 'Well, the camp shop'll be open from Easter, they'll be selling papers,' she said.

'That's weeks away,' said Bill. 'Anyway we'll be out of here by then. They'll be knocking the rest of the place to bits any day now.' He turned to look gloomily down Third Avenue and Sonia followed his gaze to the row of tumbledown prefabs that lined the narrow path; you couldn't really call it a road. The vision of the sparkling new homes that would replace them rose up before her eyes. Further away up Plotlands road, diggers were already at work.

'Destroying people's homes,' Bill said.

Sonia sighed. Some of the old buildings were nicely painted with neat gardens but others were a shambles and none of them were fit for purpose. Not in this day and age.

'Where will you go?' She fell into step with Bill as he shuffled off towards his home on Fifth Avenue.

'I'd like to go back to Lancashire. I used to have a farm there you know.' He seemed to look into the distance and Sonia supposed he was seeing his own visions. 'But Lacie won't hear of it. My daughter's trying to get us a council bungalow near where she lives in Prestatyn or maybe she'll find us a private let.'

'Oh well, that'll be nice,' Sonia said.

'How's Milly?' Bill said.

'She's okay. I'll be seeing her later.'

'Give her my regards, will you?'

'Oh sure,' Sonia said. 'This is where I turn off.'

'Pity about the shop,' Bill said as she left him standing on the corner but Sonia was already putting her earphones back in.

When she got home Sonia changed into tracksuit bottoms and sweatshirt. It was a relief to get out of the pinching stilettos and into her comfy old trainers. There was less than an hour of daylight left before supper. Sonia let herself out, bypassing the kitchen where Mrs Fairweather was busy cooking and ran joyfully to the end of Plotlands road and up onto the footpath that wound above the beach.

It was wonderful to run, feet pounding, all her body working, the air fresh and salty. She was aware of her lungs filling and emptying. The bay was beautiful, the end of the day falling into the water, a whitish mist masking the meeting point of grey sea and grey sky far, far in the distance as the tide began to turn inwards.

At first her breath came hard and her muscles complained but soon she fell into a rhythm as if she was dissolving into the landscape. Her mind was empty for a while, just feeling physical pleasure but as she began to tire, thought returned and she slowed, stretched her muscles and began to walk back, feeling the sombre note of the dying light. Darkness was crawling over the tops of the dunes as she turned onto the wooden walkway that led to the back of the Plotlands houses.

Sonia trod carefully. Last week the starry eyes of a fox had peered at her from the bushy scrub and foxes were dirty things, leaving smelly shit everywhere. Aunty Milly used to have a little Yorkshire terrier that would roll in it any chance he got and come home stinking. You had to watch out for dog poo too. Not everyone had a social conscience. There were turds all over the place, despite the convenient placing of waste bins all along the route.

189

She had her music plugged in and she was so busy looking where she was putting her feet, as she left the wooden path and crossed the rabbithole-riddled turf between the dunes and the houses, that she almost fell over the tent that suddenly reared up in front of her.

'Hey!' a male voice said and Sonia stopped as the tent wobbled and billowed before a face appeared at the opening. What a face; not Sonia's usual type, cleanshaven and polished, but a dark, craggy face, its lines blurred by soft black beard and long straggly black curls that made Sonia want to reach for a shampoo bottle.

But she looked at his eyes, green, lit with sensuality and stood fascinated for a moment before the urge to run kicked in. Then she saw that he was smiling and as well as that sensual appraisal she saw that his eyes were kind, open, nothing-to-hide kind of eyes and she relaxed a bit.

'What are you doing here?' she asked. 'This is private property.'

'Oh yeah, I forgot, Property of Questrol Oils. Ironic isn't it? They stink the place out with that monster' – he nodded towards the huge gas terminal in the distance, its nightmarish flare lighting up the spreading dusk – 'and maintain this place as a wildlife sanctuary. Salving their bloody consciences.'

'They've made it nice for people to walk,' Sonia said. 'They've even put in some natterjack toads.'

'They're not going to stay here are they? It's not their natural habitat.' He looked impatiently at her as if she was stupid.

'Anyway, you shouldn't be here,' Sonia started to feel annoyed.

'Are you going to stop me?' He smiled and her anger dissipated. 'There are more of us coming.' He wriggled and a long skinny body followed his head as he emerged from the tent flap. When he stood up he was a good six inches taller than Sonia. She liked tall men.

'I'm Zed.' He held out his hand and Sonia shook it. She felt a sexual pull in her belly which she tried to ignore.

'Zed?'

'Because I like to sleep,' he grinned. 'We don't have real names in the group.'

'Group?'

'We call ourselves, 'Habitat'. It's a joke on the shop name, you know.'

Sonia looked blank.

'We try to save natural habitats. We're going to have a protest here.'

'But this is already managed.'

'Yeah but they're building a huge housing estate here, pulling everything down. This so-called sanctuary will be reduced to a tiny strip. There'll be new roads, traffic; all the beauty of the coastline will be affected. It's not on, not on at all. You live round here?'

'Yes.' Sonia waved in the direction of Plotlands.

'Well, there you are. You're all going to lose your homes. All so those greedy bastards at Rosebrier Homes can make a fortune.'

'I'd better go,' Sonia said. 'It's getting dark.'

'What's your name?' He was looking into her eyes, that sensual look again. Sonia hoped he couldn't see her thoughts.

'Sonia.'

'Do you run every day? Will I see you tomorrow?'

'Maybe.'

'I hope so. See you then.'

'Bye.' She walked away, waited till she was hidden by a bend then sprinted homewards. Her mind was in confusion so she forgot to plug in her music and for the first time in ages she heard the night calls of the local birds as they settled in the giant Leylandi that stood at the start of the path into Plotlands.

That night, Sonia couldn't sleep for thoughts of those green eyes; not even thoughts really, just a hot racing in her blood, a tingle between her legs. Even Mike Martland hadn't produced feelings like these but it wouldn't do. She had her dreams, her future all mapped out. With Zed there would be no high heels, no smart flat. He would want her to live in a tree house and wear her hair in greasy dreadlocks. Anyway he would hate her when he found out what she was doing for a living.

The land for the first phase of building had already been cleared at the top end of Plotlands road. The choice to start there had been a sop to the holiday camp opposite, so that the work would be finished by the time the summer season was in full swing. The show house was already a breezeblock shell with a dressing of bricks up to its knees.

Sonia walked up there in her lunch hour. She'd felt restless all morning after the encounter with Zed. The solid skeleton of the show house reassured her but then she gazed over the flat wasteland that had been First and Second Avenue and thought of the people who had lived there. She hadn't really known them except for a girl called Colleen she'd sometimes played with when she'd come down to Aunty Milly's in the summer holidays as a child. But she'd got to know a few of the families in the couple of months she'd been working in the shop: the Dolans, the Wicklows, the Perkinses and the Glovers …

'What happens to the people who live here?' she asked Jim when they were having their afternoon coffee in the lull between three and four o'clock.

'They get compensation,' Jim shrugged. 'They probably get offered a council house too – I dunno. I expect they're glad to get out of this dump. I know I will be. I'm hoping to get sent to the new development up at Meliden by the golf course; now there's classy for you.'

Sonia looked at him.

'Oh, sorry, I forgot you live here don't you. But you have to agree it's not very upmarket.'

'It'll be upmarket when it's finished, won't it?' Sonia said.

'I s'pose,' Jim said, pulling an I-don't-really-think-so face. 'It's not very scenic, is it? I mean you can't see the sea for the dunes and you wouldn't want to anyway, oil and tar on the beach, not to mention those sinking sands and the view of Mostyn docks and that blinking great gas terminal. And as for that 'wildlife way' all that does is attract hordes of dogwalkers, driving up and down in their cars and leaving dogshit everywhere and what about those ponds, supposed to encourage toads? Look more like sewage puddles to me and have you heard the croaking out of them, enough to keep you awake all night.'

'It's always been a holiday resort.' Sonia found herself defending the place.

'I wouldn't come on holiday here,' Jim said. 'They only come for an afternoon out. No one comes on real holidays.'

It was true, Sonia thought. They came and filled up the car park while they had a picnic or a barbecue at the top end of the beach but by ten o'clock at night they'd all gone home, leaving the locals singing karaoke in the club and druggies and boy racers roaring up and down the road. There was the holiday camp but that was full of caravans owned by pensioners who remembered the place in its heyday; people who liked quiet walks along the dunes and who had grandchildren to entertain in the holidays. She remembered how she'd looked forward to spending her summer holidays with Aunt Milly until she got to about fourteen when the pubs and clubs of Liverpool were more attractive. She thought about Bill Wicklow and Aunty Milly who would die if she knew what was going to happen to her home.

Just then, Mike came in with some forms for her to input so that put a stop to their conversation but for the rest of the afternoon Sonia felt as if something dark was sitting on her shoulder. She took the glossy brochure for the Badger's End estate home to cheer herself up.

The tent had been joined by three others when she ran past but there was no sign of any occupants. Maybe they had gone shopping or maybe they'd gone to the council offices in Rhyl to protest about the building scheme.

Not seeing Zed made it easier for Sonia to put him out of her mind and resume her daydreams of success and luxury as she made the tedious bus journey to the home where Aunty Milly was incarcerated.

'How much am I getting for the shop then?' Milly was remarkably lucid when it came to talking about money.

'I think it's about £70,000,' Sonia said. 'I don't really know. Mum's handling that side of things.'

'Our Lally's a fool. It's worth well more than that,' Milly snorted. 'If only I could get out of here…' She looked hopefully at Sonia.

'The money means you can have your own room here,' Sonia said, 'and a little holiday now and then. That'll be nice, won't it?'

'Hmph,' Milly said. 'I'm going home. Have you got my keys? What time's the bus?'

'You need to stay here for now,' Sonia said. 'You're not well enough to go home.' No one had told Milly what was happening to the shop. It was easier to let her think it was just up for sale to a new owner.

'I'm not stopping here with all these old fogies.' Milly waved her arms at three old women slumped in front of the TV. A very old man paced up and down by the window, even though the curtains were drawn. At the sound of Milly's raised voice, he came scurrying over.

'Hello,' he made an agitated grimace. 'Hello. I do know you, don't I?'

'Hello,' Sonia said, shaking the hand he offered. 'I don't think we've met.'

He looked anxiously into her face. 'Hello. I do know you, don't I?'

'He's loopy,' Milly said. 'Where's my coat? You've hidden it.'

Sonia suffered for another half-hour, during which cocoa and biscuits provided some distraction, until she could no longer stand the overheated air with its reek of pot-pourri overlaying but not dispersing the smell of boiled vegetables and wee.

As she got off the bus, she thought of going to see if Zed had returned to his tent but it was dark and it was beginning to rain. She refused Mrs Fairweather's offer to watch TV and keep her company. Instead she got into bed with the Rosebrier Homes brochure.

She'd never realised that Plotlands had so many attractions: commanding sea views, wildlife walks, a golden beach – a setting both rural and coastal, close to local amenities, with easy road and rail access to Chester, Flint and the rest of North Wales via the A55. It seemed that the new Rosebrier Homes estate was set in the middle of Paradise. There were good local schools and doctors and plenty of leisure facilities. Sonia thought about these, she counted the two pubs and the amusement arcade but couldn't think of any others. She wondered if prospective buyers would notice that the easy rail access depended on a walk to the bus stop and a ride into Prestatyn and that the local school was also miles away in Prestatyn but then of course the kind of people who would be buying the new homes wouldn't be walking or even catching the local bus, would they?

Sonia snuggled down under the duvet as she turned to the house descriptions with delighted anticipation. Badger's End offered three different types of superior homes. The Clwyd had an open-plan kitchen-dining room with French doors in the lounge opening onto a spacious but easily maintained garden. A three-bedroomed detached property with ensuite to the master bedroom, it was a practical and attractive family home.

On the other hand, the Denbigh, a four bedroomed detached, boasted pretty bay windows, an utility room off the kitchen and an integral double garage. Perhaps a bit on the large side, Sonia thought, daydreaming about how many children she would have one day.

The Llyn was more her type of thing, at least for now. It was a two-bedroom starter home with patio

196

lounge windows and a single garage. Maybe, with a staff discount, if she got good commission, it might just be possible, if not now, then in a year or two and a house like that would still be big enough for a young married couple, even one with a small child. Happy thoughts washed through her mind as she dozed off, the brochure slipping from her fingers.

The next morning when Sonia arrived for work, she found Zed standing guard at the gateway to the building site. There was a girl with him. She had ratty blonde hair with pink and purple streaks and she wore dirty pink leggings and a greasy-looking sweatshirt. Sonia wondered if she was his girlfriend and the thought hurt her a little. She looked at the two blokes who made up the rest of the delegation: one fat, one skinny, both hairy and put her head down as she passed them, hoping Zed might not recognise her in her work clothes. Fat chance.

'Sonia?' The amazed tone of his voice matched the expression on his face when she glanced up at him. She blushed red as the tee-shirt she'd teamed with her suit and scurried into the portakabin.

'What did he say to you?' Jim demanded as she faffed around her desk, trying to calm herself. 'It's okay, I've already phoned the police, and Mike. They're all on their way.'

Sonia kept peeping out of the window. She saw the group was now waving banners that said, SAVE OUR WILDLIFE and LEAVE PLOTLANDS ALONE. She saw the blonde girl kept whispering in Zed's ear and pressing herself up against him and jealousy misted her vision. She was still fumbling blindly with the forms in her in tray when Mike Martland arrived.

'What the hell's going on?' he huffed, looking at Jim as if he should have sent them all packing by now.

'They're protesting,' Jim said.

'I can see that,' Mike said irritably.

'I've phoned the police,' Jim said.

'Well bloody well phone them again and tell them not to come.'

Jim's mouth opened but nothing came out. Sonia's vision cleared as she concentrated on listening.

'That's Matt Brierley's lad out there: the one with the greasy hair.'

Sonia fixed her gaze on the company calendar on her desk, showing the suavely smiling face of Matthew Brierley, proprietor of Rosebrier Homes.

'They've all got greasy hair,' Jim said.

Sonia didn't look up.

The police arrived quickly before Mike had managed to get hold of Matt Brierley on the phone. The girl spat at one of the officers and one of the hairy blokes was found to have a bag of grass so the lot of them were arrested and carted off to Rhyl police station. Sonia heard no more about it that day but in the evening when she went running, the tents had disappeared. She continued to run past the spot each day but they didn't return. She felt a little as if she'd lost something but she didn't quite know what.

Zed had gone up in her estimation. – someone so dedicated to his principles that he was willing to defy his own father– even though she wasn't sure she agreed with him; after all there was such a thing as family loyalty. Also, in her case, Zed's father was her employer and there was company loyalty to consider as well as the fact that all her hopes were invested in this job.

She pondered these things as she sat with Aunty Milly three evenings a week. It was good thinking time as Milly now scarcely recognised her and didn't really require entertainment or conversation. Sonia had promised her mum she would go so she continued to visit; as her mum said, someone had to keep an eye on old people in these homes or the staff might neglect them if they thought no one was bothered about them.

At work, Mike and Jim went about sour-faced. Jim stopped cracking silly jokes and only put on his cheesy smile for potential customers. Mike began taking Sonia round to different sites, once or twice a week but it wasn't till the last Friday of the month that Sonia found out the reason for this.

She was excited because Mike had come in and told her she was getting a trial at showing people round the homes on the Meliden estate on Saturday. Saturday was Rosebrier's best sales day of the week, when people were off work; there were always lots of prospective buyers. Sonia thought Mike must really be serious about training her up for sales. She would even be given a special mobile to phone the office from the showhouses.

Mike had summoned Jim into the portakabin's 'board room' and they'd been in there almost an hour during which time Sonia had posted out a few brochures to interested enquirers and made sure everything on her desk was up to date. She sat poring over the Meliden estate brochures, not wanting Mike to catch her doing nothing when he emerged. If only she had a different suit to wear for the occasion but her salary wouldn't run to it and perhaps if she wore her new pin-striped shirt, it would look like a new outfit.

It was nearly four when the boardroom door opened and Jim rushed out, face like an overripe raspberry. He pulled the drawer out of his desk and tipped the contents out on the desktop as Sonia watched, too surprised to speak.

'Getting rid of me,' he huffed, '– me – a week's notice. Bastards.'

'Why?' Sonia wanted to get up and give him a hug. He looked like a little boy about to cry.

'Unsatisfactory,' he hissed, jamming things in his pockets, 'not following instructions, failing as part of the team. It's a load of bollocks!' He slammed the drawer back in its slot. 'It's because of Brierley's lad, because I called the police. How was I to know? But then it doesn't matter,' he went on before Sonia could speak. 'Blood's thicker than water. Well, I'm off; I'm not sticking around here for a week while they all smirk at me.'

He stuffed a few papers in his briefcase, cast a look round the office. 'If you're going to stay here Son, take my advice and make sure you cover your arse.'

Sonia opened her mouth to say she was sorry but he shot out of the portakabin as Mike Martland's blocky figure darkened the inner doorway.

'Where's he going?'

'He said he's not staying.' Sonia didn't know what else to say.

'Well, don't let's worry about him.' Mike planted a plump buttock on Jim's vacated desk. 'I think you'll soon be able to step into his shoes. On Monday we'll advertise for a new junior to take over from you. You're quick enough and bright enough for better things.'

Sonia swelled with pleasure.

'It's nearly four-thirty,' Mike said, looking at his watch. 'Let's close up early and pop up the road for a drink – celebrate your promotion eh?'

Sonia remembered things her mother had said about going out with older men. She looked at the black hairs on his wrists where they poked out from his white shirt cuffs. There was something slightly wolfish about the way his tongue came out and licked his lips. Suddenly he seemed very old and she felt very young and lamb-like.

But it wouldn't do to get on the wrong side of him so she went and listened to him talking about her brilliant prospects which was interesting and listened to him slagging Jim off which was also quite interesting and then over a second half of lager, she listened as he talked about football and his twin twelve-year-old daughters which was less interesting. At least she had the excuse of having to leave to visit Aunt Milly and good enough, when he heard about Aunt Milly, he put her in a taxi like a perfect gentleman. Sonia sighed with relief and spent the journey thinking about how to cover her arse and trying to come to terms with the realisation of how insecure her employment really was.

On Saturday morning when Mike introduced her to the sales manager at the Meliden estate, Sonia's legs nearly went from under her. She reached out a hand to steady herself against the nearest desk as she stared, but she had to look and look again before she could believe what she saw.

It was Zed all right, how could she mistake those eyes? But the greasy curls and unwashed tee-shirt were gone and instead he was all clean and shiny in his dark suit with his crew-cut hair. He smelled of something expensive and he'd just the right amount of stubble to be bang on trend.

Sonia was unable to say anything in front of Mike and it wasn't until he'd gone and Zed or rather Toby, which proved to be his real name, was walking her towards the show houses that she managed to find her tongue.

'What are you doing here?' she hissed, as if Mike might be listening over her shoulder.

Toby/Zed's eyes crinkled. Sonia blushed to see he was laughing at her.

'Undercover job,' he said, taking her arm to pull her away from a large muddy puddle.

'Undercover?' Sonia had only heard the word before on television shows and her eyes widened. 'But what if they find out – your father?'

He looked at her curiously for a moment then his face cleared. 'Not undercover here. I was undercover there, with those Habitat nuts. My dad needed to find out what they were up to.'

'Oh.' Sonia felt like a soufflé taken out of the oven too soon. 'What happened to them then, the others?' She thought of the girl with the pink and purple hair and the distaste of the policewoman who pushed her head down as she put her into the back of the patrol car.

'They got let off with a caution. My dad greased a few palms.'

'Why would he do that? Weren't you – I mean they, his enemies?'

'It was all that twit Jim Fawcett's fault, calling the police out. I think they were planning to torch the building site and we'd have caught them red-handed if he'd left well alone. Thanks to that idiot Dad had to come and bail me out and that blew my cover.'

'And they didn't come back?'

'No. I think they were glad to be let off and something more important came up, some anti-fracking thing up in Lancashire.'

Sonia went into the show house in a daze. There she was introduced to Amanda whom she was to shadow for the day. Her brain scrambled further, dazzled by Amanda's impeccable hair and clothes and her wonderful flashing smile that right away made you feel she really was your friend.

When she got home that night she felt like Cinderella after the ball. She saw only the shabby cheapness of Mrs. Fairweather's home which now seemed to outweigh the comfort it had previously offered. The monotony of Sunday welled up before her with nothing to do except visit Aunty Milly and perhaps go for a run if the weather was okay. She fended it off by practising a brilliant smile in front of the dressing table mirror and internet browsing on her phone to check the prices of tooth whitening packages.

During the excitement of the day with Amanda, she'd forgotten about Zed (she really ought to call him Toby now) but as she lay in bed the two images of him came back to her; between them hung a thread of disappointment and another of hopeful ambition. She couldn't decide which one to choose and she lay sleepless for a long time until she fell into a nightmare of being wrapped up in spidersilk; a food parcel in the corner of a massive web. Only her head poked out, although her mouth was gagged with sticky cords. A trembling thrum across the web announced the imminent arrival of its monstrous creator but, gasping thankfully, Sonia woke to the mundane reality of her room.

Later that morning after Mrs F's greasy Sunday breakfast, Sonia was recovering on her bed, reading the latest issue of *Hello* when her phone trilled and her heart bumped her ribs as she saw the caller was Toby.

'What you up to?'

'Oh, nothing much,' she mumbled, tongue-tied and embarrassed in a way she wouldn't have been with Zed. She wasn't going to tell him about Aunty Milly. 'Did you want me to work today, I've got nothing on.'

'That'd be a sight for sore eyes,' Toby said and Sonia blushed even though she was fully dressed and he couldn't see her anyway. 'No, you did great yesterday by the way but you deserve the day off. I've got the day off too, wondered if you fancied coming out for lunch. I could show you round my flat afterwards. You'll love it, it overlooks the river at Chester. I can pick you up about one if you like.'

'If I like?' thought Sonia, letting the magazine slip to the floor as she got up to check her wardrobe for something to wear.

By the end of the day, Sonia's choices were made. It wasn't just the sporty car, the elegant flat, the expensive restaurant or the leisurely affluence of Chester but the presence that surrounded Toby. It was the confident way he just knew she'd accept his invitation; the way he drove as if the car was an extension of his personality and the respect shown to him, and by association to herself, by the restaurant staff and the apartment concierge. She floated home and landed with a bump in the reality of her room but something had caught fire inside her – the determination to succeed.

Six months later, Toby dropped Sonia off outside the Plotlands portakabin. The contract for the final house sale was in her briefcase and the following week she would be transferring to a new development near St Asaph where she would be trainee sales manager. The Plotlands operation was now complete.

The final client was middle-aged, wealthy-looking in a flashy kind of way. The Rolex watch was the first thing she noticed. He was quite attractive, Sonia thought, but he didn't have Toby's class.

'I hope you'll be very happy at Badger's End, Mr Graylock,' she said watching him sign the contract. Funny he hadn't mentioned a wife but he wore a thick gold wedding band.

'Call me Fred.' She blushed; he had quite a sexy grin.

After he'd gone she finished the paperwork then cleared out her desk with satisfaction. At lunchtime she took a last walk round the place that had been her former home. All the prefabs and tatterdemalion homes were gone; instead the new houses rose clean and shining in the midday sun, their pointed roofs reaching proudly to the sky. Glistening tarmac roads replaced the old cinder paths, banked by bright orange brick walls instead of the raggedy picket fences with brambles, nettles and honeysuckle rampaging through.

She did feel a little twinge when she passed the spot where Aunt Milly's shop had stood and the corner where she'd listened to Mr Wicklow complaining about the loss of the old life. But the natterjack ponds were still there, although Sonia hadn't seen any signs of the toads for a long time and the wildlife area was now a much more neatly managed park. The dunes and the beach were untouched, so really the place hadn't changed that much. The Smugglers' Rest was under new management and The Pirates' Inn had been replaced by a gastropub but that was an improvement. The amusement arcade, although retained because of the holiday camp, had been refurbished and populated with new machines to drag it into the 21st century. It was nice to see the tacky discount shop had now become a rather tasteful plant centre, Sonia thought, looking round. One improvement generated another.

She passed a clutch of the two-bed newbuilds that had been the acme of her aspirations a few months ago and she pitied that girl that she had been then; all that was before Toby had invited her to move into the riverside flat and share his lifestyle.

Now she was so happy but of course she did feel a little sadness when she thought of the old days, her childhood memories of holidays at Plotlands, now gone forever but things had to change, get better. She really ought to go and see Aunty Milly; she hadn't been at all this last month but it couldn't be tonight. Tonight Toby would collect her at five then they were going to pick up Sonia's very own white convertible BMW. It was second hand of course, but still – a Beamer – She looked down at the diamond ring on her engagement finger and admired how it sparkled back at her in the sunshine.

Lightning Source UK Ltd.
Milton Keynes UK
UKOW02f0639261116
288548UK00002B/20/P